A CHRISTMAS
Snow

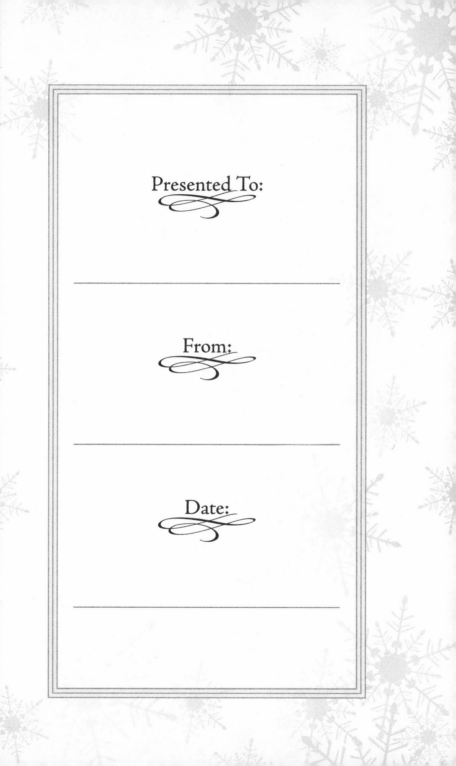

Presented To:

From:

Date:

A Christmas Snow

THE STORM OF THE CENTURY...
BRINGS THE GIFT OF A LIFETIME

A NOVEL BY
JIM STOVALL

Cover Design by: Terry French

DESTINY IMAGE® PUBLISHERS, INC.

P.O. Box 310, Shippensburg, PA 17257-0310

"Speaking to the Purposes of God for This Generation and for the Generations to Come."

This book and all other Destiny Image, Revival Press, MercyPlace, Fresh Bread, Destiny Image Fiction, and Treasure House books are available at Christian bookstores and distributors worldwide.

For a U.S. bookstore nearest you, call 1-800-722-6774.

For more information on foreign distributors, call 717-532-3040.

Reach us on the Internet: www.destinyimage.com.

ISBN 13 TP:	978-0-7684-3519-1
ISBN 13 HC:	978-0-7684-3520-7
ISBN 13 LP:	978-0-7684-3521-4
ISBN 13 Ebook:	978-0-7684-9056-5

For Worldwide Distribution, Printed in the U.S.A.

2 3 4 5 6 7 8 / 14 13 12 11 10

Dedication

his book is dedicated, first, to Dorothy Thompson, without whom this book or any of my others would not exist. It is also dedicated to her mother, Joye Kanelakos, for gracing these pages with her poetry.

And, finally, this book is dedicated to Tracy Trost and everyone involved with the movie *A Christmas Snow* and the entire project.

It is truly about the gifts, the wishes, and the message.

Surprises

Beyond the reflections
Cast on the cold ground,
Past long tree-boned shadows
This morning, I found
A field of white velvet—
Snow white—and abound
With diamonds the bright sun
Had sprinkled around.

I ran for a vessel
To gather my gain.
A fortune to cushion
All want and all pain.
But when I returned there
I sought it in vain
For the warm sun had stolen
My jewels back again.

From the personal diary of Joye Kanelakos

Introduction

 Christmas Snow has become more than a book or a movie to me. It has become special in many ways. I have written 15 previous books, and all of them are unique. I have written autobiographies, success books, business books, and novels that have been turned into movies.

A Christmas Snow was initially a story in the form of a screenplay by Tracy Trost. I wrote this book as that screenplay was being turned into a feature-length motion picture. As an author, this has been a very special journey and a rewarding process.

If you haven't already, I would encourage you and your family to enjoy the movie version of *A Christmas Snow* as well as this book. I had the privilege of being the co-executive producer on the movie, which allowed me to get somewhat involved in the scripting process, the production efforts, as well as the promotion of the film.

I have worked on movie projects based on my own books in the past, and it is a very special thing for an author to be part of his words coming to life onscreen.

If you saw the 20th Century Fox film *The Ultimate Gift* based on my novel, you may know that I played a small cameo role as the limousine driver. When you read this book, you will notice a brief scene with another limo driver near the end of the story. When you watch the movie, you will notice I, once again, am the limo driver.

As a blind person, it has been ironical for me to play a limousine driver in the movies. There are other books of mine being considered as motion picture projects, and I hope to be the limousine driver in all of them.

It may seem strange to people that a blind person like me is involved in making movies. For over 20 years my company, the Narrative Television Network, has made movies and television accessible to the 13 million blind and visually impaired Americans and millions more around the world.

I am pleased to say that when people play the DVD of the movie based on this book, it has a narration sound track option so that millions of blind and visually impaired people and their families can enjoy the movie.

When I could read with my eyes as you are reading printed words on this page, I am embarrassed to admit that I was not an avid reader. In fact, I don't know that I ever read a whole book, cover to cover. After losing my sight at age 29, I have enjoyed reading an entire book almost every day, thanks to a high-speed tape player and the National Library for the Blind. This has truly changed my life and made me appreciate reading and writing books. For this reason, I am very pleased and thankful to the people at Destiny Image Publishers that this book is available as an audio book for people like me and many others who simply enjoy the listening experience.

In addition to this book and the movie of *A Christmas Snow*, there are many other tools and resources that can benefit you and your family as you build your own Christmas traditions. Please take the opportunity to visit www.AChristmas Snow.com.

This story is about Christmas gifts, hopes, and wishes. It chronicles the journey of one family who comes to understand the gifts that Christmas represents. My hope is that you enjoy *A Christmas Snow* as a book and a movie but, even more, that you and your family will begin to embrace the Christmas wishes and gifts intended for us all.

JIM STOVALL
2010

Chapter One

he snowfall that blanketed the town that particular year became legendary and was special for several reasons. First, the snow that year was light and fluffy. It fell in huge, artistic flakes that painted the entire cityscape and countryside like a carpet of diamonds. It was nothing like the annoying wintry mix that people in the town suffer through each winter, made up predominantly of black ice and gray sleet pellets, covered by mountains of drifting frozen snow.

The snow that particular year was special for one other very important reason. It fell at Christmastime.

A white Christmas is not just something that people in Minnesota sing about or watch in movies. It is an ordeal they annually struggle through. It makes decorating and holiday shopping a chore while inflicting hardships on friends and family trying to visit the area or residents attempting to travel out of town for holiday celebrations elsewhere.

The snow that fell that year was not accompanied by sleet or ice. It arrived just before Christmas, was easy to get around in, and wondrous to look at. That magical snow signaled to everyone that it was going to be a special Christmas that year.

The traditional Christmas songs sung by strolling carolers seemed to have a little more hope and energy than previous years. The Christmas lights were brighter, and each decoration seemed new and pristine like the wonderful snow.

This was especially true at the Mitchell residence, a white, ranch-style home where

10-year-old Kathleen was convinced that the holiday this year was certainly better than anything contained in her previous Christmas memories. She was decked out in her snowflake pajamas and lying on the floor, gazing up at the glorious Christmas tree that was arranged in front of the picture window in the Mitchell living room.

Like the snow, the tree this year was simply better than ever before. It boasted strings of popcorn she had created herself, along with an assortment of garlands, some new store-bought ornaments, and some of her family's traditional hand-crafted decorations. A star glistened from the treetop, and everything seemed to be in its place.

It was all special to her, but Kathleen's absolute favorite was the solitary white porcelain angel ornament she had prominently displayed on the exact, perfect branch of the Christmas tree.

Kathleen was lost in her thoughts of holidays past and what promise the bright and shiny packages under the tree might hold for her.

Her reverie was broken by the angry voices of her parents' current argument that drifted to her through the open doorway of their bedroom. Their hostility and vicious words blended with the background Christmas music, creating a macabre symphony and an ominous ballet. Although Kathleen tried to ignore it, these verbal battles between her parents had become more frequent and more vicious in recent days.

Kathleen sighed deeply and tried to refocus her attention on the beautiful Christmas tree. She crawled under the branches to try to gain a new perspective and escape from the increasingly intrusive sound of her parents' argument invading the living room. Kathleen shut her eyes and tried to focus on the magical Christmas celebration that she had been looking forward to ever since she had finished her last piece of Thanksgiving pumpkin pie.

Her holiday thoughts were interrupted by the sound of her father's approaching solid footsteps. She rolled over and opened her eyes in time to see his strides, punctuated by a swinging suitcase, as he passed the Christmas tree, opened the front door, and solidly slammed it behind him with finality.

Kathleen had seen her father leave the house many times and for many reasons, but deep down in her soul, she knew something was different today.

She leapt to her feet and gazed out the picture window as her father crossed the snow-covered yard. Kathleen knocked on the window, and her father stopped and turned so he could look over his shoulder and see her framed in the window with the backdrop of the Christmas tree behind her. Then, without expression, he deliberately turned and simply walked away.

As Kathleen watched her father's back retreating into the snow and dark night, a single tear rolled down her cheek and fell.

Chapter Two

lthough three tumultuous decades had come and gone, Kathleen still remembered that long-ago glistening tear as a drop of water fell into her bathroom sink. She gazed into the bathroom mirror before her, looking upon what other people thought was her stunning face; but as usual, her expression was firmly closed off, and she simply didn't give much away.

The 40-year-old image that gazed back at her did not please her, not because she didn't like it, but because that kind of thought or emotion would have to reach Kathleen at a place she had closed and locked 30 years before.

Just then, a timer buzzed, and Kathleen removed a teeth whitening strip, rinsed with water, inspected her already impeccably white teeth, and grimaced. She opened her color-coordinated medicine cabinet and loaded her toothbrush for one more cleaning.

Kathleen's entire life was made up of a series of daily routines and rituals.

A few minutes later, as was her custom, Kathleen dressed in her color-coordinated jogging suit that was the latest fashion in sports-wear, with her iPod strapped to her arm and her ear buds in place.

Over the years, and especially each winter, she was glad she had left Minnesota far behind, along with its Arctic weather and painful mem-ories. Here in Tulsa, Oklahoma, you could run outdoors virtually year 'round.

Kathleen managed to jog her regular route through the neighborhood and around a nearby park without noticing any of her neighbors waving at her or the wonderful scenery around her. She just put one foot in front of the other until she was back in front of her house.

She slowly walked across her yard as her breathing calmed and her heart rate approached normal. As she moved along her front walkway and approached the front porch, she saw the morning newspaper perched on the front steps.

Kathleen turned off her iPod, took out her ear buds, and reached down for the morning newspaper. As she held it in her hand, she saw her own picture staring back at her from the corner of the front page of one of the sections of the paper. She looked at her own image that she had known would be there. She looked away and walked into her house.

Kathleen marched into her kitchen and threw the paper onto the counter. It landed with her picture staring at her once again from the top corner. She began loading an assortment of fruits, juices, and various powders into her blender. She hit the button, and the blender whirred into action. Only then did Kathleen allow her attention to move back to the newspaper lying on the counter.

She concluded her normal morning routine in the kitchen with the paper closed and her picture staring at her the whole time. As usual, she was in control of her emotions, and whatever was in the newspaper about her would simply not be allowed to affect her resolve.

Only when Kathleen was completely ready for work according to her usual high standards did she walk into the kitchen, finally opening the newspaper to reveal what was inside. She removed Sections A and B, which she immediately tossed into the recycling bin, leaving Section C, the Food and Wine Section, laying open before her.

On the cover of the Food and Wine Section of the morning newspaper, there was a picture of Kathleen with an uncomfortable expression on her face. She was holding a turkey. The bold headline read, NOT QUITE HOME FOR THE HOLIDAYS. Kathleen immediately refolded the section of the newspaper and tossed it into the recycling bin to join the other discarded sections.

Even though she had decided she wouldn't give them the satisfaction of reading the article or letting it affect her in any way, a short time later she found herself furiously scrubbing a drinking glass full of soapy water in the sink as she stared at the now-soiled front page of the Food and Wine Section on the counter beside her.

Kathleen was so distracted by the newspaper that she absentmindedly picked up the glass of soapy water and took a big drink from it. She gagged and let out a frustrated cry as she stormed into the bathroom to brush her teeth once again.

As Kathleen went into her autopilot mode and rapidly backed her car out of her garage and into the street, she failed to notice a delivery truck stopping in front of her house. The driver hopped out and rushed onto the porch. After ringing the doorbell repeatedly, he left a small brown package beside Kathleen's front door.

As Kathleen drove to work that day, she spread open that same Food and Wine Section of the morning newspaper across her steering wheel. At a red light, she read the vicious words and exclaimed aloud to herself, "Comfort food has never been so cold."

Just then her cell phone rang, and she picked it up. She answered automatically without checking the caller ID, knowing that it had to be someone from work calling about the newspaper article. Without saying hello or uttering a greeting of any kind, she stated, "I'm reading it right now. And, no, it doesn't mean we're closing for Christmas."

Kathleen heard an uncomfortable silence on her cell phone followed by the bewildered and unexpected voice of her mother repeating, "Hello. Hello?"

Kathleen refused to let the usual flood of emotions created by her mother's voice wash over her. She simply closed the phone and tossed it onto the seat beside her. She was so distracted that she did not notice the light had changed or anything else until the phone on the seat beside her insistently rang again.

The caller ID confirmed to Kathleen that her mother was persistent that morning. She ignored the ringing phone and accelerated through the intersection. She couldn't deal with the multitude of emotions and feelings, so, as usual, she simply blocked them out and drove to work.

Chapter Three

ulsa, Oklahoma, is a unique community. Depending upon whom you speak with, Tulsa is either a large town or a small city. It has many of the amenities and features of a world class metropolis, but people tend to know each other or at least know people who know people, like a small town.

Kathleen drove without thinking along her standard route into downtown Tulsa and parked her car in her usual parking space. As she walked down the sidewalk, she spotted the sign on the awning outside her business that proclaimed *Kathleen's Ti Amo's Restaurant*. It was a classic Italian eatery housed in a beautiful 1940s era brick building. Most people would feel a sense of pride or accomplishment as they walked beneath such an awning on their way to work each day. The most Kathleen could muster was a mild sense of satisfaction as she walked through the front door of her restaurant that morning.

As she entered, the early morning crew was busily cleaning up and getting everything in readiness for the luncheon crowd. The second that everyone became aware of Kathleen's presence, the fun and camaraderie among the employees disappeared. Kathleen's presence was like a wet blanket that dampened the spirits of all who made their living at *Kathleen's Ti Amo's Restaurant*.

If Kathleen was aware of this, she gave off no sign of recognition. She simply acknowledged everyone present with a monotone, "Morning."

Her greeting was met with absolute silence until Martin, a heavyset man of 50, mustered the courage to respond. "Good morning, my dear."

Kathleen cut to the chase: "I know you've read it, so you can stop with all the pleasantries."

Martin, feigning innocence, asked, "Read what, my dear?"

"The article in all of the newspapers I'm sure you hid when I walked in." Kathleen held out her hands and demanded, "C'mon, hand them over."

A guilty-looking busboy pulled a paper from beneath a table cloth.

Martin looked at the newspaper Kathleen now held in her tightly clenched fist and said, "Oh, yes. *That* newspaper."

Kathleen nodded emphatically. "Yes, *this* newspaper."

Martin presented a peace offering, saying, "It's really not so bad."

"They called me a Gourmet Grinch. I've never read so many bad puns in my life." Kathleen glared.

"It's just the small town mentality. Everyone should be with their families on Christmas."

"We're like a family. Right?" Kathleen inquired of everyone. The staff fell completely silent.

Chef Claud, a round man of 42, popped his head in from the kitchen. Kathleen looked at Claud for the answer to her question. "Right?"

Claud shrugged and said, "I guess. Like a dysfunctional family."

"Who never goes on vacation," Martin chimed in.

"Funny," Kathleen shot back sarcastically.

Martin smiled. "Almost as funny as this." He handed her a note.

Kathleen sighed in frustration. "Ugh. My mother is relentless."

Martin pursed his lips. "Shouldn't you just talk to her? She said it was urgent."

Kathleen waved it off. "It's just her annual Christmas invitation."

"It really wouldn't hurt to close the restaurant for a day," Claud inserted.

Kathleen shook her head definitively. "Not a chance. I have mouths to feed."

Martin and Claud exchanged knowing glances and, finally, Claud mumbled, "Not after that article."

"I won't abandon all of our loyal holiday loners," Kathleen said emphatically. "Besides, how…"

Martin and Claud completed her sentence in unison. "How can we feed them if we aren't open?" They both laughed.

Martin looked at Kathleen. "Then we'd better rethink your Christmas gift."

"Oh, yeah?" Kathleen shot back.

Martin responded, "We were all gonna pitch in to change the locks."

Kathleen appeared frustrated as she crumpled up the phone message from her mother.

Martin and Claud laughed again, and Claud sighed in relief and said to Martin, "Whew! I could kiss you."

Martin got a mischievous look on his face and said, conspiratorially, "Speaking of which…" as he walked to his maitre d' stand and pulled out a branch of mistletoe. He snuck up behind Kathleen who was busy looking over the day's reservations. As he moved in close, Kathleen demanded, "Stop."

Martin began making kissing sounds.

Kathleen turned around and said, "Stop that. What in the…" She sighed and continued, "If you don't put that away, I'm gonna…"

Claud interrupted saying, "What? Have some fun? You're a prude."

Kathleen shot back, "Yes, I'm a prude. A Christmas prude. Now get back to work."

As Kathleen walked toward her office, Martin whispered to Claud, "She's the prude who stole Christmas."

Kathleen said, "I heard that," as she continued walking to her office.

Martin cleared his throat and addressed all of the employees in the dining room, announcing, "Half hour until doors open."

Chapter Four

owntown Tulsa boasts a smorgasbord of architecture. There are the same type of new steel and glass monstrosities evident in any major metropolitan area, and then there are some marvelous art deco buildings that are holdovers from the oil boom and the wealth that flowed in the first half of the last century.

At midday, workers rush out of these buildings to try to get a brief bite of lunch during their limited lunch hour or to have a more leisurely meal while discussing business with prospects or colleagues.

Kathleen had always taken a great deal of satisfaction from the fact that her restaurant had a great reputation with the lunch crowd. People could either get in and out quickly while still having some quality food or linger over a multi-course meal while doing business.

The dining room was full once again, and Martin was deftly making his way from table to table, greeting diners and making sure everything was up to Kathleen's high standards.

Kathleen had retreated to her office where she was trying to deal with the myriad of emotions that were competing inside of her head. Without thinking, she unwrapped a chocolate Santa Claus. She took a calculating look at the chocolate holiday figure before she viciously and thoroughly bit Santa's head off and began chewing.

Martin stuck his head through her office doorway. Kathleen greeted him with "Go away, I'm hiding."

Martin persisted, "I think you might want to see this."

Kathleen moved over to the open door where Martin stood, and followed his gaze toward a table across the dining room where the food critic who had written the awful newspaper review was casually seated.

"What's he doing here?" Without waiting for an answer, Kathleen charged toward the table, blurting out, "You've got a lot of nerve coming to my restaurant after that review."

The food critic looked up at her calmly and said, "Why, Kathleen. Your food is great. There's just no Christmas cheer in here."

Kathleen was about to let him have it, but Martin interceded to save the other luncheon diners from hearing her forthcoming verbal onslaught. "Um, Kathleen. You have a call holding."

Kathleen glared at the food critic and tried to dismiss Martin. "Tell her I'm busy with a customer."

"It's not your mother."

Kathleen's attention was diverted away from the vengeance she was planning to inflict on the food critic as she turned curiously toward Martin.

"It's a handsome gentleman caller," Martin explained.

Kathleen's countenance and entire attitude immediately changed. "Andrew! I could use some good news today."

Giving the food critic one more threatening glare, Kathleen turned and strode toward the bar, where she picked up the phone and said without any greeting, "Please don't tell me you're calling to cancel."

Across town, Andrew—a handsome businessman—was sitting at his desk in his office as he responded, "Not canceling...but there's a little change of plans."

Kathleen gripped the phone tightly and said, "So, you've read the article."

A loud chuckle was all the response she got from Andrew before he said, "No. In fact I'm bringing you more business."

Kathleen inquired curiously, "Oh, yeah? How much more?"

He responded, "Just one other person—my daughter."

Kathleen grimaced and tried to keep some of the frustration and trepidation out of her voice, "Oh. That's great."

The magical dinner she had been planning in her restaurant that night with Andrew, and the special evening she was anticipating after dinner, disappeared into thin air like a mirage in the desert.

Chapter Five

athleen had always insisted that her staff transform *Kathleen's Ti Amo's Restaurant* each evening from an efficient and inviting lunch spot into a wonderful, upscale Italian eatery. This exquisite transformation had once again taken place, and some of the dinner patrons began arriving at Kathleen's restaurant.

Kathleen herself was seated at the best table in the house, where she had planned to dine with Andrew Wright, the recent object of all of her affections and hopes for the future. Andrew was dressed as a stylish businessman should be, out for an important but casual evening. Kathleen had come to expect that Andrew would dress appropriately for any situation. What she had not expected was that Andrew's 10-year-old daughter, Lucy, would be joining them for the evening.

Lucy had spread her napkin on her lap and was doing the same thing for her father, who failed to notice her efforts. Kathleen instantly realized she had forgotten to place her own napkin in her lap, and she knocked over the salt shaker as she nervously corrected her error. She quickly righted the salt shaker and clandestinely brushed the spilled salt into her lap as the waiter approached.

If Andrew had noticed Kathleen's blunder, he ignored it as he cheerfully noted, "Food's here."

Kathleen scrutinized each of the plates carefully, as the waiter stood by nervously, hoping for her nod of approval.

She seemed pleased and turned to Andrew, saying, "I hope you like what I picked. I had Claud make it especially for you."

Andrew responded by digging into his meal. "Oh, wow! This food is amazing."

Kathleen baited him for an additional compliment, "You really like it?"

Andrew nodded enthusiastically as he was still chewing and trying to swallow a large bite. He nudged his daughter, encouraging her to pay her compliments as well, "Lucy, don't you think this looks amazing?"

Lucy's only response was to stare in bewilderment at the plate before her.

Kathleen trod lightly, asking, "Is everything okay?"

Lucy responded as if confronting a space alien. "What is *that?*" She glared at a gourmet hamburger with a museum-worthy garnish and an assortment of dipping sauces.

Kathleen answered timidly, "Um, it's the Kobe Beef burger. It's organic."

Lucy moaned and announced, "I can't...I just... I can't take it...." Lucy began to breathe heavily as if she were going to hyperventilate or pass out.

Andrew turned to his daughter with all the parental tone he could muster, commanding, "That's enough, Lucy."

JIM STOVALL

Kathleen leaned toward Andrew and inquired, "Is she okay?"

Before Andrew could respond, Lucy blurted out dramatically, "Get it away!"

"We discussed this. Now is not the time," said Andrew.

"Are you okay? What's the matter?" Kathleen asked Lucy.

"I'm a Chicketarian," Lucy responded.

Kathleen was bewildered. "A what? A chick..."

Andrew turned to Kathleen and explained, "A Chicketarian. It's new."

Lucy continued as if speaking to a preschooler. "I don't eat meat. Except for chicken."

Kathleen was flustered. "Oh, I'm sorry. Do you want something else?"

Andrew answered for Lucy saying, "She's fine," but Lucy countermanded, saying, "Uh, yeah," assuring Kathleen that the only reasonable course of action was to bring her another meal.

Kathleen looked back and forth between Andrew and Lucy, unsure whose lead to follow. Lucy simply took out her cell phone and began to text. Then she announced offhandedly, "I need to eat."

"How about a chicken salad sandwich?" Kathleen cheerfully offered.

Lucy dismissed that notion. "Hate it."

Andrew packed all of the ominous warning that any parent can put into saying a child's name aloud. "Lucy."

Kathleen encouragingly offered an alternative. "Chicken tenders?"

Lucy rebuffed her again. "I had that for lunch."

Kathleen was wracking her brain for something she could feed this troublesome child, but she wasn't doing well under the pressure. Without thinking, Kathleen said, "We have a nice chicken fried steak."

Lucy's eyes narrowed as she turned them on Kathleen like a judge questioning an uncooperative convict. She inquired, "Are you trying to trick me?"

Kathleen blushed as she had not immediately realized her mistake.

Andrew reached over and took the phone from his daughter. He admonished her again. "Okay, Lucy. That is enough."

Trying to keep her emotions in check, Kathleen said, "Maybe I should go talk to the chef." She pushed away from the table and headed toward the kitchen.

Andrew called after her, "Kathleen, don't worry about it."

She turned and unconvincingly said over her shoulder, "No, really. I want to." Feigning a sweet smile, she continued toward the kitchen.

Andrew turned to Lucy. "What is wrong with you?"

Lucy blurted out, "She's so…."

Andrew prodded her, "So what?"

"So NOT Mom," Lucy explained with finality.

Andrew realized that his daughter had put into words the problems he was having in his life with both Lucy and Kathleen.

Chapter Six

hef Claud was the master of his domain. He had always understood, as did everyone who worked for Kathleen, that she was thoroughly and firmly in charge of the restaurant; but once you crossed the threshold and entered his kitchen, he was the king.

Kathleen burst through the door as Claud was putting the final touches on a dessert masterpiece. It was more a work of art than food.

Kathleen announced, "That child is unbelievable." She grabbed a piece of the chocolate dessert from under Claud's hands. As she absentmindedly started eating it, Claud rolled his eyes and began working feverishly to repair the damage. He said calmly, "She's cute."

Kathleen shoved more of the chocolate dessert into her mouth. "She's a Chicketarian."

Claud shrugged nonchalantly, but Kathleen confronted him, "And don't pretend like that's normal." She continued, "Hey, what's the grossest thing we have that looks like chicken?"

"Maybe you should ask Andrew."

"What?" Kathleen spun around and was surprised to see Andrew standing in the kitchen doorway.

Kathleen was embarrassed and flustered. "I'm so…" She wiped remnants of the chocolate dessert off her mouth with her sleeve. "I am sorry and embarrassed."

Andrew was apologetic. "Don't worry about it. I mean, *I'm sorry*. She's a mess tonight. This time of year is hard on her."

Kathleen was uncertain how to respond or what to do. She patted Andrew on the shoulder, but her action seemed to intensify the discomfort between them.

"Hey, it's okay," Kathleen said, resignedly.

Andrew repeated, "I'm sorry about all of this."

Kathleen tried to soothe him. "Don't be."

Andrew tried to explain. "It kind of sneaks up on you." Then Andrew seemed to shake off his sadness, and his countenance lightened.

Kathleen sensed his improved mood and asked, "Is there anything I can do better? You know, to help."

Andrew smiled at her in amusement. He had noticed that Claud had become engrossed in their private conversation. "I don't know. What do you think, Claud?"

Claud turned red and looked like someone who had gotten caught with his hand in the cookie jar. Andrew laughed, but Kathleen was still pensive.

Andrew smiled and said, "Kathleen, you're great. And Lucy's really great, too. I really need you to see that. Just promise me you'll give her a chance."

Kathleen nodded with more encouragement than she felt.

"Please order her a corn dog."

Kathleen began to protest. "But…"

Andrew put a finger to her lips, interrupting her. Then he grabbed a napkin and wiped the remaining crumbs from Kathleen's face. "Believe me. The kid can't resist a corn dog."

Andrew and Kathleen made their way back to the table where Lucy did, indeed, later devour an entire corn dog.

Kathleen asked, "How was it?"

Lucy sat the corn dog stick back on her plate and answered noncommittally, "Fine."

Andrew turned to Lucy encouragingly and asked, "What do you say?"

Lucy responded perfunctorily, "Good night, Kathleen." The young girl reached for her coat and began to put it on. Andrew looked at Kathleen apologetically. When Lucy stood up, she dropped her napkin on the floor.

Andrew warmly addressed Kathleen with a simple, "Thank you."

He turned to Lucy and said, "Thank you was the answer I was looking for from you."

Lucy just rolled her eyes.

Kathleen ignored the awkward moment. "Sure you can't stay for dessert?"

Andrew was torn, but stood as if to leave. "I'd love to, but I still have some packing to do, and I have to drop Lucy off with her sitter."

Lucy interjected, "I don't need a sitter."

Andrew ignored Lucy's protest and said to Kathleen, "But I'll drop by your place on the way to the airport."

Kathleen responded, "Sounds good. We can have dessert then."

Andrew gave her a coy wink, saying conspiratorially, "Okay, then."

Kathleen blushed brightly and gave a nervous glance toward Lucy who was oblivious to the conversation as she buttoned her coat to leave. Flustered, Kathleen said, "I didn't mean…"

Andrew chuckled and gave her a kiss on the cheek. Then he turned to Lucy and commanded, "Lucy, thank Kathleen."

Lucy mumbled in a monotone voice, "Thanks," and moved toward the door.

Andrew got his coat and followed his daughter, calling over his shoulder to Kathleen, "Don't forget the dessert."

Kathleen blushed again and picked up the napkin Lucy had dropped. She wondered if there would ever be a way to work out this frustrating triangle that included Lucy, Andrew, and her.

Chapter Seven

K athleen was somewhere between a workaholic, a micromanager, and a total obsessive-compulsive. Total focus on her work had made her successful through the years, and it had also provided her with a welcomed distraction from her past as well as her lack of a personal life.

Once again, she was working alone in her office at the restaurant. She was pouring over facts and figures, orders, supplies, and tax information. As usual, her total focus had caused her to completely lose track of time when Martin poked his head in and said, "Hey boss, you're the last one out."

Kathleen shook her head distractedly and tried to redirect her attention, simply uttering, "What?"

Martin's interruption had brought her back to the present. She snapped to attention, checked her watch, and realized she was running late for her upcoming rendezvous with Andrew before he left for the airport. She began gathering her things in a mad rush.

She closed her office door and hurried into the restaurant's kitchen. She absentmindedly tossed all of her things on the counter and opened the refrigerator in search of the dessert she had promised Andrew, or at least one form of dessert he was expecting. She opened one of the boxes in the refrigerator to reveal a meringue pie.

She held the pie box deftly in one hand and loaded up all of her possessions strewn across the counter in a complex balancing act. In the midst of her balancing act, she overlooked her cell phone, which remained on the kitchen counter as she rushed out of the restaurant.

Normally, Kathleen's commute home from the restaurant took 18 minutes. She had timed it on many occasions. But as she pulled into her driveway, she noticed with a little satisfaction—and relief she had not been stopped by a police officer—that she had made it home in a little over 12 minutes. She pulled her car into the garage and rushed into the house as the garage door automatically lowered.

In her bedroom, Kathleen stood in front of a full-length mirror observing her image in a form-fitting top. She tried to assume a model's pose, but it came off more awkward than seductive. She knew the top wasn't right, so she rushed into the closet to survey the possibilities.

Over the next few minutes, a number of articles of Kathleen's clothing were taken off their hangers, quickly tried on, and then hurled out of the closet to land haphazardly in her otherwise pristine bedroom. Just as a blue sweater rocketed across the bedroom and landed on the floor, she heard her doorbell ringing persistently.

Prompted by the urgent doorbell ringing, she hastily donned a bathrobe and then quickly tried to pick up the clothing she had strewn across her bedroom before she rushed to the front door.

On the front porch, Andrew was insistently ringing the doorbell as Lucy stood next to him. Neither of them noticed the package beside the door that the deliveryman had left earlier that day.

Kathleen only partially opened the front door before Andrew barged inside with his arms loaded with a glittering array of tulle. Kathleen had to frantically step back to avoid being run over by Andrew and the glittering mesh fabric.

Andrew blurted, "I've been calling like crazy."

Lucy entered the open door in her father's wake carrying a craft kit and a backpack. She looked down at Kathleen's bare legs beneath her robe and pointed out matter-of-factly, "She's not wearing pants."

A feeling of dread settled over Kathleen as she suddenly became aware of her attire. She followed Andrew into the living room, becoming conscious of her clothes she was still holding. She quickly hid them behind pillows on the sofa.

Andrew inquired in a businesslike manner, "Do you sew?"

Kathleen was taken off guard, and asked, "Do I what?"

Andrew explained, "Sew. You know, needle and thread?"

Kathleen was further distracted as she noticed Lucy had made herself at home on the sofa with the remote control. Kathleen turned back to Andrew and admitted, "Uh, no."

Lucy informed her father, "You can't leave me with a pants-less woman."

Andrew scolded her, responding, "Enough, Lucy."

Andrew began stacking Lucy's things on Kathleen's table.

The terror of the situation began to dawn on Kathleen, and she asked Andrew, "Leave her here? What happened to the sitter?"

Andrew shot back, "She cancelled on us."

"Obviously." Lucy echoed the tone of her father's explanation toward Kathleen.

Andrew looked at Kathleen with pleading eyes and said, "It's just one night."

Before Kathleen could respond, Lucy cut her off with a threat. "A lot can happen in a night."

Andrew knelt down in front of his daughter and said hopefully, "You guys are gonna have fun. Think of it as...girl time."

Lucy responded incredulously, "Really?"

"I'll be back before you know it."

"In time for my show?" Lucy asked.

"Wouldn't miss it," Andrew answered reassuringly. "And I bet we can convince Kathleen to save me a front row seat."

As Andrew stood up, Lucy simply rolled her eyes.

Andrew turned to Kathleen and asked pleadingly, "Do you mind?"

The expression on Andrew's face told Kathleen that this was a complex situation with a lot at stake. She took a deep breath and responded, "Of course not."

He smiled with relief and maybe a little bit more. "You're a life saver."

Lucy asked, "But what about my costume?"

Andrew answered more toward Kathleen than Lucy. "Kathleen will take care of it. Right?"

Kathleen stammered, "Uh...right. You need it *tomorrow?*"

Quick good-byes, hugs, and kisses were exchanged, and Andrew rushed off for the airport.

A few moments later, Kathleen was in her kitchen with Lucy standing atop an upturned stock pot, facing her and holding colorful fabric around her waist. Kathleen was on her knees trying to thread a needle.

Lucy commanded, "Hurry!"

Kathleen responded with more patience than she felt, "Don't rush me."

Lucy explained, "I kinda have to."

Kathleen mumbled with the needle between her lips, "Technically, we have until tomorrow night."

"But I need time to practice in it. I'm the star."

"I thought you were an angel."

"Duh," Lucy shot back. "But I'm also the star of the show. Besides, I have to go to the bathroom."

Kathleen abandoned the needle and thread in frustration and declared, "Okay. New plan."

Lucy responded, "Great."

Kathleen fished two safety pins out of the craft kit and asked, "Do you have any more safety pins?"

Lucy gave her a blank look as she dropped the skirt to the floor and plopped onto a nearby chair.

Kathleen stood and responded, "Well, I'm gonna have to pick some up."

Lucy followed Kathleen into the living room and plopped down on the sofa as Kathleen picked up her car keys. Lucy turned on the TV.

Kathleen said, "Come on. Get your coat. We have to go to the store."

Lucy responded, "You can go without me. I'll be fine."

Kathleen protested, "I don't think that's a good idea. Your dad put me in charge, and I can't just leave you here."

"Yes, you can," Lucy explained. "My dad does it all the time. I'm 10 years old. I'm not a child."

Frustrated with the situation, Kathleen said, "I really think you should come with me."

Lucy was already glued to the television screen. "This is my favorite movie."

Kathleen glanced at the black and white Christmas movie on the screen and asked doubtfully, "It is?"

"No," Lucy responded, "but you should go. The store closes at midnight."

Kathleen stammered, "But…," and realized she was waging a losing battle. She shrugged resignedly and grabbed her purse. "I'll be back in 15 minutes, tops."

Lucy never took her eyes away from the TV screen. "'Kay."

Kathleen called a final warning, "Don't budge from that sofa."

Lucy was engrossed in the movie and repeated distractedly, "'Kay."

"Actually, you should probably get ready for bed."

Lucy responded again automatically, "'Kay."

Kathleen uneasily left through the doorway, muttering, "Um, okay."

Finally alone, Lucy began surfing channels.

Chapter Eight

s Kathleen piloted her modest powder blue sedan down the street toward the supermarket, she couldn't help but notice how deserted the Tulsa streets were as midnight approached. She flipped on the radio absentmindedly and struggled to gain some visibility by wiping the foggy windshield.

She heard the voice of Steve Smith, a sound familiar to most Tulsa residents, floating out of her car stereo speakers. "A cold front is passing through…"

Steve Smith was generally a fixture in morning radio, but when weather emergencies threatened Tulsa, you could hear his voice at any time of the day or night. He continued, "…on its way from the west for the holidays."

KBEZ radio had a new policy of playing Christmas music 'round the clock for many weeks leading up to the holiday. Steve Smith intoned, "So here's a little something to get you in the mood," as a rendition of "Let It Snow" began to play.

Kathleen spoke aloud to the radio, "Seriously." She could not imagine anyone voluntarily listening to Christmas music, much less doing it for weeks on end.

Kathleen reached into the glove compartment and fumbled for a napkin to wipe more of the moisture from her windshield. Later, she would be certain that she had only looked down for an instant, but when she looked back up to the road in front of her, her headlights revealed an elderly man standing in the middle of the road directly in front of her car.

Kathleen stomped on the brakes reflexively.

Her tires squealed on the pavement as her car continued to skid forward. Everything moved in slow motion, and the next few milliseconds seemed to stretch out for hours. Kathleen's car finally shuddered to a stop with her bumper a mere inch from the man standing in front of her.

Kathleen laid her head on the steering wheel, thinking she had hit the old man. Finally, she gained the courage to sit up and assess the damage her carelessness had caused.

Startled, she exclaimed, "Oh!"

The man stared at her through the windshield. The two of them shared a moment of eye contact as the reality settled over Kathleen that somehow she had not hit him. She mouthed the words, "I'm sorry," as a weak offering of apology.

The old man simply nodded his acceptance and walked away toward the bus stop on a nearby corner. Kathleen blinked, took several deep breaths, and finally eased her foot off the brake and drove onward.

Somehow, she was able to steer her car down the road to the entrance to the supermarket parking lot. She turned in and pulled into a parking space. Her car was the only one in the parking lot at this late hour.

She got out and rushed into the deserted store.

The supermarket was quiet except for the constant buzz of the fluorescent lights and the same rendition of "Let It Snow" blaring out through the tinny supermarket speakers.

Kathleen rushed down the craft aisle and grabbed safety pins, pipe cleaners, and some glitter for good measure. Out of nowhere, a disheveled teenager wearing a Santa hat rocketed past her on a skateboard.

Kathleen shouted, "Hey! Watch it!"

The teen laughed loudly as he continued on down the aisle. Kathleen regained her composure and took a quick inventory before adding some super glue to her basket, just to be safe.

Finally, she felt that the ample supplies she had amassed should be sufficient for any contingency she might face in assembling Lucy's costume.

She rushed toward the checkout aisle, but there was no cashier in sight. A fat Santa figurine holding a calendar that proclaimed *December 20* seemed to be staring at her questioningly. Kathleen was unsettled by Santa's dubious gaze, so she reached out and turned the figurine so he would be facing away from her.

She looked the length of the counter and was confronted by a stack of newspapers, all displaying her picture staring back at her.

Kathleen heard the sounds of a scuffle near the front door and glanced over to see a scrawny, mid-30s store clerk forcefully escorting the teen with the skateboard and another young man out of the front door of the store. As the youths were thrust through the door, the clerk grabbed the Santa hat from the skateboarder's head. He turned and ruffled the clerk's hair. Both of the boys laughed and walked away.

The clerk was no match for the teenagers in size, but he made up for it in volume as he yelled, "Shame on you! And on your mothers!"

The clerk composed himself and returned to the register in front of Kathleen as if nothing had happened.

The clerk immediately noticed that the Santa figurine was out of place, and he rotated it back into position. He looked Kathleen in the eye and then reached for a microphone to make an announcement over the store's loudspeakers.

"Please bring your final purchases to the register. The store will be closing in three minutes."

Kathleen winced at the feedback from the speakers, but as the Christmas music resumed playing, she wondered if the feedback wasn't preferable.

Kathleen set her basket full of craft items on the counter. The clerk gave the basket a quick glance, replaced the Santa hat atop his head, and silently rang up Kathleen's purchases on the store register.

As an afterthought, the clerk looked at Kathleen questioningly as he nodded toward her purchases, saying, "Christmas party?"

Kathleen stammered, "Uh, no."

The clerk was a bit flustered as he responded, "Oh. I saw the glitter and just, you know, assumed."

"No. No party," Kathleen said with finality.

The store clerk glanced at her again. "You look familiar. Do you live around here?"

Kathleen just stared at him, and he continued pressing buttons on the cash register.

The clerk blinked. "I mean, I'm sure I've seen you before."

Kathleen shook her head abruptly. "No. Can we get on with it? I'm in kind of a hurry."

As the store clerk looked away, Kathleen flipped over the top newspaper on the stack, effectively hiding her picture.

The store clerk announced automatically, "That's $9.97. Would you like to give a dollar to the children?"

Confused, Kathleen asked, "Which children?"

The clerk, annoyed with her response, grabbed the ten dollar bill out of Kathleen's hand and quickly handed her the change. After the display of the clerk's surly attitude, Kathleen didn't dare protest.

The store clerk looked away and muttered insincerely, "Merry Christmas."

At a loss for words, Kathleen turned and walked out of the store. The clerk followed her as far as the front door, where he locked up for the night.

Kathleen was certain that this night couldn't get any worse.

Chapter Nine

athleen walked across the sidewalk in front of the supermarket and moved out into the deserted parking lot toward her car. As she walked, she rooted through her purse in search of her car keys.

Kathleen was always thoroughly organized and never misplaced anything, so she couldn't imagine why, after midnight on this of all nights, she couldn't find her car keys.

She spoke in ironic frustration. "Seriously?"

She reached her car but still failed to find the errant keys, so she began spreading the contents of her purse across the car's hood. She took a mental inventory of her purse's contents spread before her. As she was realizing that everything seemed to be there except for the car keys, she heard the sound of skateboards approaching from behind.

The two teenagers from the store stopped beside her. These youths, merely annoying inside the store, now seemed more ominous. One of them inquired, "Need some help?"

Kathleen blurted out a bit more frantically than she intended, "No, thanks. I'm fine." She tried to ignore them and hurriedly began replacing each of the items that had been spread out on her car hood back into her purse.

The young man spoke again, asking, "Did you lose something?"

Kathleen heard her own voice, and it seemed high-pitched and panicked as she said, "No. I'm good. You can go. I'm fine. Thanks." She forced a fake smile and tried to feign being calm.

The two young men leaned on the front of her car casually. The one who had spoken before said, "Ya know, I'm really good at finding things."

Kathleen tossed the last of her things into her purse, but still could not find her keys. She turned to walk away from the two young men, but the one who had been questioning her stopped her in her tracks. Before, he had only been annoying, then threatening, but now he was being forceful.

"Come on, lady. Now you're just being rude. You don't want to be rude, do you? It's Christmas."

He reached over to take her purse. "How about you let me carry that heavy bag for you." He yanked at the purse, spilling its contents all over the parking lot. "Now look at what you did," he said, accusingly.

Suddenly, the old man that Kathleen had nearly run over appeared out of the darkness at the rear of her car. He spoke assertively, stating, "In my day, when a lady asked you to leave her alone, you left her alone."

The teen who had grabbed Kathleen's purse spoke dismissively to the old man. "How about you just mind your own business and go back to your shelter."

"Fun's over," the man shot back confidently. "Now just go on home, and leave this nice lady be."

The teen stepped between Kathleen and the old man and patted the man on the face condescendingly. "Like I said—this is none of your business, old man."

Quicker than Kathleen would have imagined, the old man grabbed the teenager by the neck and squeezed until the youth's face began turning red. The old man hissed, "I'm making it my business."

The second teenager spoke from the shadows where he had been looking on. "Let him go!"

He ran toward the old man and raised his skateboard as if to use it as a weapon. He swung the skateboard wildly and hit the man on the side of the head.

The man slumped to the pavement and lost consciousness.

The teenagers disappeared into the darkness.

Kathleen rushed to the man's side and said, frantically, "Mister, mister. Are you okay?"

The man groaned and moved, beginning to regain consciousness. He could see Kathleen leaning over him through the fog in his head. He echoed her question. "Are you okay?"

Kathleen smiled ironically. "Am *I* okay? Are *you* okay? You took a nasty hit."

"No, no. I'm fine." He started to get up.

Kathleen wasn't sure what to do, so she began organizing the mess that the spilled contents of her purse had made. As she haphazardly picked up each item and shoved them one-by-one into her purse, she noticed a bus pulling away from the bus stop on the corner.

The old man also looked at the bus moving away and then glanced back at Kathleen as she frantically searched through her belongings. "Did you lose anything?"

The old man helped recover several of Kathleen's things, and as he brought them to her, she noticed a red mark on the side of his head, just at the hairline.

Kathleen said, "I just…I don't know…I just need to find my keys." She continued rummaging through her purse and said, "I can't find my phone, either. I need to call the police."

The old man responded quickly, "No, no police. I mean...please don't call them on my account. I'm fine." He seemed nervous.

Kathleen put a hand in her jacket pocket, reaching for her phone, but found her car keys instead. She began to feel calmer and took a closer look at the old man's head. "You're hurt."

He reached up and touched his head. "Nah." He picked up his hat where it had fallen on the parking lot, put it back on his head, and declared, "There. All better."

Kathleen smiled and fidgeted with her keys, uncertain what to do next. She said, "I'm so sorry. I almost ran you over."

"Yes, I guess you did," the man agreed.

"I'm very sorry. I should have said something earlier."

The old man shot back, "That's quite all right, Kate. It's Kate, right?"

Kathleen took a step back and looked at him questioningly.

The man's eyes smiled in amusement. He explained, "It's there on your coat."

Kathleen looked down. She was wearing a coat with her restaurant logo on it. She moved her scarf to reveal her full name and was almost embarrassed.

"It's Kathleen, actually."

"I stand corrected. Kathleen then."

Kathleen said, "Right. Well, there you have it. Thank you for your help."

The old man reached out to shake her hand and said, "Sam."

Kathleen shook his hand. "Sam, well, hopefully we'll never meet again." She nervously laughed at her own bad attempt at a joke.

Sam seemed baffled. "Excuse me?"

"I mean, hopefully I won't run into you again. You know, the car...." At his blank look, Kathleen gave up on her failed explanation and moved to get into her car, saying, "Well, okay then. Merry Christmas."

Kathleen quickly closed her door and started the car. The rush of adrenaline that she had experienced during the incident faded away, and she felt chilled. She turned on the car's heater and backed out of the parking place to drive home.

Chapter Ten

Kathleen had always prided herself on being organized, unemotional, and in control of her environment. She had lived this way in her personal and professional life for so many years that it was part of her. She felt that, if you controlled everything outside of yourself, you didn't have to let anything in; and, therefore, if you never let anything inside, nothing could hurt you. This almost always worked for Kathleen, except for that night.

The confrontation in the supermarket parking lot had shaken her badly. On top of all the other turmoil she had dealt with that day, it was almost more than she could take. She tried to compose herself as she drove toward the supermarket parking lot exit.

As she was driving out of the parking lot, she noticed the old man, Sam, standing at the bus stop on the corner. She looked at his battered briefcase and worn-out trench coat and felt a wave of remorse come over her.

Kathleen pulled back into the parking lot and drove toward the corner just behind the bus stop. She rolled down her window and called out, "Uh, Sam, can I give you a ride somewhere?"

Sam pulled a pocket watch from his coat and took a look at it. He seemed to be considering his options when a cold gust of wind made up his mind for him.

He said, "Well, it appears that I have missed my bus. I could use a ride to the bus station."

Sam got into the passenger side of Kathleen's sedan, and she pulled out of the parking lot and drove toward the Greyhound bus station, which was a few blocks away in the heart of downtown

Tulsa. They arrived at the bus station at 12:30 A.M., but not a soul was in sight, and the ticket center was closed.

Sam looked at the darkened building and declared, "Well, this doesn't look promising." He spotted a sign and said, "According to the sign, they are closed. Looks like my bus is gone."

Kathleen asked, "When is the next one?"

Sam glanced back at the sign. "It says the doors open at six A.M."

As Sam opened the passenger door of the car to get out, Kathleen glanced down at the digital clock on her dashboard, noticing that it was 12:35 A.M.

Sam said, "I'll be fine. You go on home."

"Where are you going to sleep?"

Sam looked around the outside of the deserted bus station. "I can make myself comfortable just about anywhere."

"It's freezing," Kathleen protested.

Sam shrugged. "I have a coat."

Kathleen took a deep breath, made up her mind, and said, "You're coming with me. It's my turn, anyway."

"Your turn?"

"I almost killed you. You saved my life. The last thing I should do is let you die in the cold."

Sam just smirked and got back into Kathleen's car.

They sat in awkward silence on the drive back to Kathleen's house. Kathleen pulled the car into the garage and let Sam follow her inside. She led him through her kitchen and was painfully aware of the fact that she now had a stranger in her home for the night.

She said, "I'll have to put some sheets on the guest bed." Kathleen turned on the light and walked to a tidy linen closet in the hall.

Sam said, "You didn't mention you had a daughter."

Kathleen was confused until she remembered Lucy was also a house guest for the night. "Oh, I don't...Oh, my goodness. I can't believe I forgot about her."

Sam seemed bewildered. "You forgot you had a daughter?"

Kathleen stammered, "No, no. She's not my daughter. I hardly know her. I mean, I'm just watching her for someone."

Sam looked at the little girl asleep on the sofa with a halo hanging crookedly from her head. "She looks…worn out."

"Good," Kathleen responded.

Sam gave her a questioning look.

Kathleen explained, "She's been difficult to deal with." She gathered a pile of sheets and towels in her arms.

Sam said, "I can take it from here. Just point me in the right direction."

She handed him the sheets and towels and pointed the way down the hall, saying, "It's right here." She directed him to an open door just off the dining room.

Sam nodded. "Okay. Good night then."

"Night," Kathleen responded as she watched him disappear into the room and close the door behind him.

Kathleen turned and walked into the living room. She noticed the TV was still on. As she reached for the remote to turn it off, she saw a news report announcing that a major snowstorm was on the way.

Kathleen turned toward Lucy, who was fast asleep on the sofa. The three shirts that Kathleen had hidden behind the cushion were now folded neatly on the arm of the sofa. Somehow, Lucy's thoughtful gesture bothered Kathleen. She was not used to being caught off guard. She snatched up the folded clothes and tried to wake Lucy, but she wouldn't budge.

Kathleen finally scooped Lucy into her arms and carried her toward her own bedroom. As they moved down the hall, Lucy wakened enough to scold Kathleen. "You're late."

Before Kathleen could even respond, Lucy was fast asleep once again.

Kathleen deposited Lucy's inert form onto the bed. She walked over and closed the bedroom door and rested her head against it before she locked the door from the inside. She reached into her closet to put away her shirts that Lucy had folded and emerged to find Lucy sprawled across the entire bed, dominating all of the sleeping space.

Kathleen tried to move Lucy to one side of the bed or the other. In frustration, Kathleen finally gave up and resigned herself to sleeping on a pile of blankets on the floor.

Chapter Eleven

ften, people's homes are a reflection of their lifestyle or personality. Kathleen's home was no exception. It was neat and pristine and would remind a visitor of a furniture store display. Everything was artfully and tastefully arranged, but there was little or no personality revealed within the living space. Kathleen had always liked it that way.

She awoke the next morning and instantly felt out of sorts. She immediately realized that she had slept on the floor beside her bed, and the events of last night came into her memory.

The bright sunlight streaming through the window blinds alerted her to the fact that she had overslept. She checked the alarm clock on her nightstand, but it was off. She tried the table lamp sitting next to it, but it wasn't working either. She came to the conclusion that there was no electricity in her house.

She had a sinking feeling as she looked at her now-deserted bed. Lucy was gone. Kathleen began to imagine the worst possible explanation.

She called out, "Lucy?"

Kathleen rushed toward her bedroom door. She had carefully locked it last night, but now her bedroom door was ajar. She pulled it open and entered the hallway, trying the hall light switch, which had no effect.

She called out again, "Lucy?"

As she continued down the hallway, she heard a scream from the end of the hall.

"Lucy?!"

Kathleen became brutally aware of the gravity of the situation. She had a small child in her house who was no longer protected behind the locked bedroom door, along with a strange man whom she knew nothing about other than the fact that he had single-handedly fought off two attacking teenagers the night before.

Kathleen reached into her hall closet in search of a suitable weapon. All she could find was an umbrella. It would have to do. She grasped it in her hand and moved assertively to the end of the hall. She heard another squeal as she rounded the corner into her kitchen.

Kathleen demanded, "Okay, hold it right there."

She was not prepared for the scene before her. Lucy was seated at the counter, and Sam was standing at the counter, preparing mugs for hot chocolate. Both Sam and Lucy immediately turned toward Kathleen and stared in confusion.

At the sight of Kathleen holding the umbrella in front of her, Sam stated matter-of-factly, "You're gonna need more than that today."

Kathleen struggled for the right words. "Huh? What? Why didn't you wake me up?"

Sam and Lucy just continued staring at Kathleen.

Kathleen questioned, "What time is it?" As she looked at Lucy, she continued. "You're late for school."

Lucy responded offhandedly, "School's canceled."

"Canceled?"

Lucy replied, "Yeah, look outside."

Kathleen drew back the curtain and peered out the window. She was not prepared for the scene before her. It was a winter wonderland. The snow was piled up past the windowsills, and it was still coming down in big flakes.

Sam said, "Looks like last night's cold front was an ice and snow storm."

Kathleen began rummaging through her purse again and said, "I can't find my phone. I've looked all over." She began to retrace her steps through the house, searching for her errant cell phone.

"You don't have a phone here at the house?" Lucy asked.

Kathleen kept looking as she answered, "No, just a cell phone." At last, the realization hit her. "And I left it at the restaurant."

Sam and Lucy exchanged a knowing glance.

"I'll just have to go get it."

Sam responded, "I don't think you should go out there."

Kathleen waved dismissively, "C'mon. How bad can it be?" She walked to the door that led to the attached garage. She pushed the button to activate the automatic garage door opener, but nothing happened.

Sam followed her into the garage and said, "Here. We can raise it if we release it from the opener." He reached up and pulled down on a cord which extended from the base of the electric garage door opener. He stepped over to the garage door and lifted, but it was stuck and wouldn't move. He gave it several more strenuous pulls until it broke loose from the ice at the bottom with a thud.

Kathleen and Lucy stood on either side of Sam, looking on as he raised the garage door. Kathleen picked up a cheap plastic shovel.

Lucy looked at the mass of snow and ice revealed by the open garage door and then turned to Kathleen and said, "I don't think you're going to get out of here."

Kathleen spoke to no one in particular. "I need my phone."

Lucy kicked the icy layers of snow to demonstrate their plight.

Kathleen spoke with determination. "I'll just have to dig."

"Let me help you," Sam offered.

Kathleen turned to Sam and said, "You just relax inside. I'll let you know when we're ready to leave."

Kathleen had a huge smile plastered on her face, which totally baffled Sam.

Chapter Twelve

eople from many parts of the coun-try regularly confront large piles of snow blocking their driveways. The sight that confronted Kathleen as she stood in her garage looking at the deep snow that ran all the way to the street would not have appeared unusual to many people, but it was unusual in Tulsa.

The snow that confronts Oklahomans each year is made up of as much ice and sleet as actual snowflakes. It often freezes into a hard, solid mass.

It can look like a picturesque, fluffy snowfall, but in reality, it forms a concrete-like barrier.

People in Tulsa are usually thankful that this wintry precipitation doesn't get more than an inch or two deep, but the frozen wall that confronted Kathleen had drifted several feet deep and loomed as a formidable and significant obstacle.

Kathleen stood in front of the deep snow clutching her plastic snow shovel.

Sam suggested, "I think we might be better off…"

Kathleen smiled and clutched her shovel even tighter. She dismissed Sam's offer, saying, "I insist."

Sam didn't dare argue with a woman holding a shovel. He shrugged. "Well, holler if you need me."

Sam moved toward the door into the house, and Lucy followed him.

Kathleen called, "Lucy, why don't you wait out here with me?"

"No, it's freezing," Lucy shot back.

Kathleen insisted, "Well, do jumping jacks. Run in place. I don't care what you do. Just do it out here."

Lucy was stunned by Kathleen's harsh demeanor. She stood in place, not knowing what to do next. Her 10-year-old mind couldn't grasp the potential danger that Kathleen feared Sam might pose.

Lucy whined, "Can I at least get my backpack so I can read?"

Kathleen just nodded and replied, "Yes, but come right back out."

Lucy huffed and retreated into the house.

Kathleen picked up the plastic shovel and attacked the snow. As she confronted the mass in front of her, with a loud thud her shovel broke into many pieces.

Kathleen moaned and said, "Seriously."

Lucy returned with her backpack and sat on the stairs that led from the house down to the garage floor. She took out a book and began to read.

Kathleen would not be daunted by the defective plastic shovel. She went into the house and returned with great determination and an array of kitchen utensils. She began attacking the frozen snow with a meat cleaver. She made a small dent in the pile but did not even approach the progress that would be required in order to get her car out of the garage. She looked over at Lucy and paused to get her breath.

"Whatcha reading?"

Lucy did not even look up as she answered, "A book."

"Really. What's it about?"

"A vampire woman who holds little girls and old men hostage and threatens them with butcher knives."

"So, it's a love story," Kathleen responded, determined not to let this 10-year-old get the best of her.

Lucy cracked a smile, and Kathleen took the meat cleaver in hand and got back to work.

Sam appeared at the garage door and announced, "Okay. All the food from the fridge is in the cooler now."

Kathleen was out of breath from her hard labor. "You really...didn't...have to do that."

Sam smiled and tried to reassure her. "I want to help. Can I make you guys breakfast?"

Lucy perked up and squealed, "Pancakes!"

"Nothing too messy," Kathleen warned.

Sam held back a smile so as not to offend Kathleen. She looked like a complete and utter mess after her strenuous labor. "One batch of not-too-messy pancakes coming right up."

As Sam headed back inside, Kathleen took a deep breath and mustered the strength to continue digging.

Lucy pleaded, "Can I go in and help him?"

"Fine. I don't care what you do."

As Lucy got up to follow Sam into the house, the distinct sound of a cell phone ringing came from her backpack. Kathleen froze her digging efforts in mid-chop.

Chapter Thirteen

athleen feared she might be in a state of delirium from her extreme efforts in attacking the frozen snow with nothing more than kitchen utensils. At least she knew her sanity was intact when Lucy reached into her backpack and pulled out a cell phone. "Hello?"

Kathleen stared open-mouthed. She was about to explode as Lucy calmly reached into her backpack again, retrieved a magazine, and began to peruse it as she talked on the phone.

"Still snowed in. No. He's inside. And his name is Sam. Uh-huh, he's real nice. But Kathleen doesn't like him."

Kathleen could only hear a soft murmur from the other end of the phone conversation.

"Yeah, she finally woke up. 'Kay."

Lucy paused and held the phone out to Kathleen. "My dad wants to talk to you, and he doesn't sound too happy."

Kathleen dropped the meat cleaver, took Lucy's cell phone, and walked inside the house with the young girl trailing along. "Hello?"

Kathleen quickly updated Andrew on the situation they were facing. She tried to reassure him that Sam was okay and not someone they needed to worry about. As she considered her own words, she wondered if they were true.

As Kathleen walked into the kitchen, Sam flipped a golden brown pancake through the air, and it deftly landed on a plate. Sam slid the plate along the counter as he ladled another spoonful of pancake batter into the skillet on the gas stove. A couple of drops of batter fell onto the counter, and Lucy pointed and warned, "You better wipe that up."

Sam smiled and wiped up the batter with a paper towel.

Lucy watched Sam flip another pancake, and she declared, "You've got moves."

He chuckled and replied, "That's nothing. I'm an amateur."

"I'm very mature for my age," Lucy exclaimed, "but I can't do that."

Sam smiled as Lucy eyed the plate of pancakes. He set it aside on the counter. Lucy pulled a chair over to the counter and climbed up onto it to confront the stack of pancakes now before her.

"Is that for me?"

Sam explained, "That plate is for the first person who asks politely."

Lucy rolled her eyes and tried again. "May I please have those pancakes?"

"Yes, you may, young lady."

Lucy climbed down from the chair, curtsied, and carried the plate to the table. She looked up at Sam. "Syrup?"

Sam gave her a stern look.

Lucy smiled and tried again. "I mean, syrup, please?"

Sam presented a bottle of maple syrup to her with a formal bow. Lucy sighed. She said under her breath, "Manners."

Sam heard her and responded, "Never go out of style."

Lucy looked at Sam seriously from top to bottom. "I never hung out with an old person before." She took a big bite of pancakes. "But you're funny. You know...for an old guy."

Sam considered her remarks. "I'm gonna go ahead and say thank you."

"Just to be polite?" Lucy asked.

Sam nodded and sat down across the table from her. He finished the thought. "Yes, manners."

Lucy smiled and slid the syrup over to him.

Kathleen couldn't think of eating pancakes, given their current predicament. She retreated to the darkened bathroom and laid down fully clothed in the empty bathtub with her feet propped up on the wall to continue her conversation with Andrew in private. She tried to explain Sam's presence. "I don't know how many times I can apologize. I will try to get him out of here as soon as I can."

She listened to Andrew's response through the cell phone. "Who knows when that will be. The whole town's shut down." Kathleen banged her head on the tile wall behind her in frustration.

Alarmed, Andrew asked, "What was that? Where are you?"

"Hiding in the bathtub, and I was banging my head against the wall."

She heard Andrew chuckling on the other end of the line. He tried to recover by quickly saying, "Sorry. That's not funny."

Kathleen sounded snippy as she shot back, "You're right. So stop snorting."

Andrew resumed laughing and said, "You're in some state of mind. Serves you right!"

"I lend a helping hand, and this is what I get."

Andrew just laughed harder, and Kathleen sat up in the bathtub and got serious, saying, "Okay, that's enough. We have a cell phone battery to preserve. Call me when you find out about your flight."

Andrew warmed and said, "Take care."

"You, too," she responded softly.

Andrew inserted one last thought. "And Kate..."

"Yeah?"

"Don't talk to any more strangers."

"Very funny."

She hung up the phone, and just when she thought things couldn't get any worse, Kathleen moved to climb out of the bathtub and accidentally hit the faucet handle with her foot. Freezing water shot out of the shower head, instantly drenching her from head to toe.

Chapter Fourteen

he snow and ice that encased the city of Tulsa, Oklahoma, paralyzed all normal activities in the community. Some people were stranded at home, while others were stranded away from home. For some people, it was a hardship bordering on a tragedy, while others enjoyed a fun and significant time spent with friends and family.

Whether people were suffering hardship or enjoying the white Christmas was partly a matter of circumstance, but greatly determined by each individual's attitude.

Kathleen's scream at being drenched by cold water from the shower reached Sam and Lucy, who were busy in the kitchen. They had both determined it was best to keep busy and stay out of the way so as not to intrude on Kathleen's private call with Andrew.

They were washing the breakfast dishes, and at the sound of Kathleen's scream, Lucy turned to Sam and said offhandedly, "Sounds like a breakup to me."

Sam tentatively suggested, "Maybe you should check on her?"

"Do you really think she wants to see me right now?"

Sam nodded, seeing the wisdom in young Lucy's question. He echoed her sentiments. "We'll give her a few minutes."

Kathleen struggled out of the bathtub, got some fresh towels out of the hall closet, and dried off. As she held Lucy's cell phone in one hand and towel dried her damp hair with the other, she thought it was ironic that she looked and felt better than she had all day.

Kathleen walked into the living room and collapsed onto the sofa to relax for a minute.

Lucy's head popped up from the back of the sofa, and she reached over and grabbed her cell phone out of Kathleen's hand.

Lucy inquired cheerily, "Nice chat?"

Kathleen closed her eyes to block out Lucy and try to refocus her thoughts. She responded calmly, "Yes. Thanks for asking."

Sam called from the kitchen, "We saved you some pancakes."

"No, thanks. I'm not hungry."

Lucy addressed Kathleen with enthusiasm. "You gotta try them. Sam's a genius chef. I mean, he really knows how to cook."

Kathleen's eyes popped open in realization. She stared at the cell phone in Lucy's hand, and said, "I need that back."

Lucy argued, "For what? I don't think my dad wants to talk with you again."

"I need to call *my* genius chef."

"Well, I'm bored," Lucy bargained. "Find me something to do, and you can use my phone."

Kathleen motioned, and Lucy followed her down the hall to an almost-forgotten storage closet. Kathleen opened the door and shined a flashlight inside, revealing a mess of boxes, games, toys, and other odds and ends.

Lucy exclaimed, "Oh, my gosh! I love vintage."

Kathleen sighed and rolled her eyes.

Lucy gazed at the wonderful treasures that jammed each shelf and asked, "Where did you get all this stuff?"

Kathleen shrugged and answered, "Life, I guess."

Lucy began rummaging through the shelves, exploring all of the hidden mysteries. She scooted aside an Easy Bake Oven and picked up a wig head. "Weird life."

Kathleen shrugged, knowing deep inside that Lucy was totally accurate with her assessment.

Kathleen dismissed the topic, saying, "You have no idea." She pointed her flashlight toward a particular shelf and said, "The games are here."

Lucy set down the wig head and rushed toward the shelf illuminated by Kathleen's flashlight. A number of board games were revealed.

Lucy considered the possibilities. "Hmm."

Kathleen impatiently tried to prompt Lucy. "Pick something, would ya?"

"You have somewhere to be?" Lucy shot back sarcastically.

Kathleen thought of her predicament. "I have important calls to make."

"On my phone," Lucy argued.

"Hey, you called the deal."

Lucy sighed thoughtfully and pulled out a worn edition of *Don't Break the Ice*.

"I want this one."

Kathleen scrunched her face. "Really?"

"It's a classic!"

Kathleen held out her hand and commanded, "Phone."

Lucy rolled her eyes and reluctantly handed over her cell phone. "You're like a child," she admonished Kathleen, who just stared at the 10-year-old. Lucy turned and walked out of the closet, clutching the game.

As Kathleen closed the storage closet door, Lucy skipped down the hall carrying the board game. Kathleen turned in time to see one of the plastic cubes fall from the board game box. As Kathleen bent to pick it up, in her mind she was transported back to a time over a quarter of a century before.

Chapter Fifteen

ur memories are not totally fact or completely fiction. They are a conglomeration of the thoughts that we put together to explain to ourselves who we are. Just like a beautiful flower garden will look totally different in daylight as opposed to in the dark, the memories of our past are held hostage by our perspective.

Kathleen had edited the images from her childhood to create the person she had become.

In her mind, she was once again 13 years old and picking up off the floor one of the plastic game pieces from *Don't Break the Ice*. She was in her childhood home with her mother and her new stepfather. The three of them were playing the game on the coffee table, and pieces of the "plastic ice" were strewn across the table.

Young Kathleen replaced the piece that had fallen on the floor.

As more pieces scattered across the table, Kathleen's mother exclaimed, "Whoa!"

Kathleen resumed her spot, sitting on the floor in front of the coffee table, directly across from her mother and her mother's new husband, Bill, who were seated side by side on the sofa. Bill Mitchell was a balding man of 45 who had recently come into their lives and tried to fill a role that Kathleen was convinced he never could.

Bill announced enthusiastically, "Okay, Katie. Looks like it's down to you and me."

Kathleen solemnly corrected her stepfather. "It's Kathleen."

She wouldn't even look Bill in the eye. Whenever she was forced to speak to him, she would look at her mother or simply avert her gaze in another direction.

Kathleen impatiently inquired of her mother, "May I be excused?"

Kathleen's mother looked uneasily toward Bill. Her expression carried the weight of the difficult transition of trying to blend a new family with a new husband.

Kathleen's mother forced a cheery expression onto her face. "Honey, it's family night. C'mon, let's just finish the game."

Assuming her normal role as the peacemaker and focal point of this fledgling new makeshift family, Kathleen's mother placed her hand tenderly on Bill's and said to him, "She is really good at this game. She beats me every time we play."

Bill feigned a doubtful expression and challenged Kathleen, saying, "This I have to see."

Kathleen rejected the challenge, pursed her lips tightly, and shot Bill a steely glare.

Bill shifted gears. "But maybe some other night. It's getting late."

Kathleen's mom gave Kathleen a pleading look to no avail. The girl ignored both adults and began methodically packing up the pieces of the game. Bill and Kathleen's mother sat solemnly and watched her.

A feeling of helplessness came over them. They wanted to reach out and touch Kathleen or soothe her in some way, but Kathleen did not want to be reached or touched. She was long past being receptive to those kinds of thoughts and emotions. She deflected every caring and loving gesture away from her and used them to build the wall around her higher and thicker.

She didn't want to think about the past other than to hold on tightly to her anger. She didn't want to feel anything in the present, because those feelings led to the open wounds from her past. She didn't want to believe in the future or hope for good things, because she felt life had already taught her that those things weren't possible for her.

Suddenly, in her mind, the grown Kathleen came back to the present. She was standing in her own hallway, holding the plastic game piece that had dropped from the box Lucy had carried down the hall.

Kathleen was shocked at how vivid her memories were from that long ago game of *Don't Break the Ice* with her mother and stepfather. Somehow, she knew that—even though she was a grown woman and a successful business-person—the scared, confused, and angry 13-year-old was alive and well, deep inside of her.

Chapter Sixteen

eople who live in Tulsa, Oklahoma, in the 21st century may think they still have the pioneer spirit lingering inside of them. While they may, indeed, retain the spirit of their pioneer ancestors, most Tulsans have lost the skills and practical knowledge to survive day-to-day life without modern conveniences.

Due to the winter storm, people all across the city were dealing with the lack of phones, electricity, and heat. Their immediate discomfort would give them a new appreciation for the everyday conveniences that their pioneer ancestors would have considered miracles.

Sam and Lucy had settled into Kathleen's breakfast nook, where Lucy was busy setting up and organizing her newly-adopted favorite game, *Don't Break the Ice*. She looked up at Sam and speculated, "I imagine you'd like to play with me."

Sam looked down at the mysterious pieces of the game. He found *Don't Break the Ice* baffling, as he had never played the game before. "You, my dear, have quite an imagination."

"My therapist says I use it to cope," Lucy responded.

"Yeah? What do you think?"

The question made Lucy ponder. She had many confused thoughts, but finally found the thread of an answer that suited her. She turned to Sam and started to explain. "I think it's...like a lollipop."

Sam was bewildered with her analogy. "A lollipop?"

Lucy continued as if it were the most logical idea on earth. "Yeah. Like at the doctor's office.

After you get a shot, you get a lollipop, and it makes the pain go away."

Sam looked at Lucy reflectively, and he considered the implications of her answer. He probed further. "You've gotten a lot of shots in your life, haven't you?"

Lucy nodded and agreed, "Yeah."

Sam locked eyes with the 10-year-old who had obviously seen more of life's difficulties than her first decade should have brought her. They were kindred souls. "Me, too."

Lucy responded, "I know."

"Oh, yeah? How can you tell?"

"You have a good imagination."

While Sam and Lucy were trying to understand life and the game in front of them, Kathleen was sitting at the desk in her home office. A binder was spread out in front of her. Each of the sections within the binder was meticulously marked with individual colors, creating a tidy rainbow effect.

She found the phone number she was searching for and efficiently dialed it on Lucy's cell phone. The phone rang several times, and then Kathleen heard a familiar voice answer on the other end.

She said, "Martin! Great. Please tell me you are at the restaurant." Kathleen glanced out the window. "No, I'm stuck, too. I wanted to talk about the Christmas menu. I mean, this can't last all week, can it?"

The cell phone began beeping. Kathleen didn't wait for Martin's response. She frantically exclaimed, "Ughhh. The phone is dying. So plan on being open Christmas and please don't give me a hard time about it. I'm not in the mood."

Kathleen immediately snapped the phone shut to preserve any battery power that might be left. She slammed the binder closed in frustration and blurted out, "Shoot!"

She could hear Lucy's squeal of delight as Sam and Lucy, still in the breakfast nook, engaged in a heated game of *Don't Break the Ice*.

Sam accidentally broke the ice with the hammer. He cried, "Oh!"

Lucy tried to console him. "Don't feel bad! I used to play this with my mom and dad all the time."

Sam smiled. "I might have rethought this if I knew I was going up against a pro."

"You think I'm a pro? You should've seen my mom. She was great. I don't think I ever saw her break the ice."

"Sounds like she's got the touch."

Lucy shook her head wistfully. "There was no one like her."

"Was?" Sam questioned.

Lucy spoke as if she were carrying the weight of the world, "Yeah."

"Where is she, if I may ask?"

"She's gone."

"Gone where?"

Lucy considered for a moment. "Heaven, I think." She busied herself fiddling with the pieces of the game.

"I'm sorry to hear that. I know it's tough to lose a loved one."

"It's the worst. But how do you know?"

"I'm old. Trust me. I've lost my share of people along the way."

"They all died?" Lucy inquired innocently.

Sam shook his head. "No. Some of it was my own doing."

Lucy's eyes widened in terror. She looked over at a block of knives on the kitchen counter.

"Wait a second! You're not, like, a serial killer, are you?"

Sam was shocked by her response. "What? No!"

"But you said…"

Sam explained patiently, "I meant it was my fault. Like I drove some people away. I'm not a killer!"

Lucy shot back, "That's a relief 'cause I don't approve of that."

Kathleen picked that moment to walk into the breakfast nook and stand behind Lucy and Sam.

She asked, "Approve of what?"

"Murder," Lucy explained.

Kathleen walked past them into the kitchen where she began rummaging through drawers in search of a lighter.

She responded to Lucy's comment about murder, "Well, good. Neither do I."

"You know what else I don't approve of?"

Kathleen inquired, "What's that, Lucy?"

Lucy glared at her sternly. "Stealing."

Kathleen was confused, but Lucy clarified, "My phone, Kathleen."

Kathleen was flustered but recovered, saying, "Oh, um, it's in my office. I was hardly stealing it."

Lucy got up and began to walk out of the room. She announced, "I'm calling my dad to make sure he's okay."

Kathleen snapped, "Make it quick. The battery is almost dead."

Lucy strutted out of the room, leaving Sam and Kathleen alone. Sam gestured toward the game on the table and asked, "Want to play a round?"

Kathleen looked down at all the pieces and wrinkled her nose. "Oh, I don't think so. I'm not a big fan of that game."

Chapter Seventeen

ll of us carry our own individualized brands of grief and sorrow. Shallow people believe they are the only ones who have ever felt the anguish they have experienced. Deeper people have learned that the human condition is defined by the collective pool of pain that we all dip into. Only when we try to understand one another's suffering can we begin to bring each other joy.

Lucy had fled her uncomfortable and revealing conversation with Sam. She rushed into Kathleen's home office and climbed on the desk chair. She found her cell phone lying on Kathleen's desk, picked it up, and dialed her father. The phone beeped, signaling a low battery. It continued to beep intermittently as the phone rang.

Lucy snooped through Kathleen's desk drawers as she waited for her father to answer. She stumbled upon a small lollipop hidden in the back of one of the drawers. She toyed with it as she heard the phone answered on the other end and spoke questioningly, "Dad?"

She heard her father's familiar and reassuring voice. "Hi, honey."

Lucy was all business, cutting right to the chase. "Who do you like better? Mom or Kathleen?"

The silence stretched out over the phone line. Finally Andrew spoke. "Lucy..."

Lucy continued. "You know you can't replace her."

Andrew tried to reassure her. "I know, honey. She was special."

Lucy corrected her father, saying, "She *is* special."

"So is Kathleen."

Lucy retorted, "But she's special in a bad way. She has no Christmas decorations in her house."

Andrew implored, "I want you to give her a chance. Please."

Lucy sat in silence.

"Lucy?"

Lucy sighed resignedly. "Okay, fine. When are you coming home?"

The phone gave one final beep before it died completely. Lucy sighed and closed the phone. She took a lick of the lollipop, but she did not like the flavor, so she put it back in its wrapper and replaced it in Kathleen's drawer where she had found it.

As Lucy sat and reflected on her mother, her father, and Kathleen, Sam and Kathleen were in the breakfast nook, engaged in a heated game of *Don't Break the Ice*.

Kathleen tapped precariously with the hammer on the fragile sheet of plastic ice as Lucy reentered the room.

Sam leaned over the table expectantly. "Easy," he instructed.

Kathleen spoke to the game imploringly, "Come on, baby. Light as a feather."

Lucy began chanting like a cheerleader. "Concentrate. Concentrate."

Kathleen glared at her. "I can't concentrate with you talking!" She gave one last tap, and the plastic polar bear crashed through the ice. Kathleen violently shoved the pieces aside. She spoke in frustration, "Oh! Come on! This is a stupid game!"

Sam began gathering the pieces to put the game away. Kathleen scowled at him, but Lucy began giggling and said, "You've lost it."

Lucy's giggles spread to Sam, who tried to keep it under control.

Kathleen tried to act as if she were offended, but she began to get a case of the giggles, too.

Sam spoke through his laughter. "In all my years, I never would have thought…"

Kathleen interrupted, "Are you kidding me?"

Sam continued, "Stuck inside. What a Christmas."

Kathleen chimed in, "And with strangers, no less."

Lucy's mood was the first to sober. She looked out the window forlornly and asked, "Do you really think we'll be stuck here for Christmas?"

Sam matched her mood and gazed out the window, saying, "By the looks of it, it's a possibility."

Lucy pursed her lips and sighed heavily, announcing, "I hate this Christmas."

Kathleen agreed, "Welcome to my world."

Lucy looked at Kathleen and said emphatically, "But I don't want to be like you." She began to cry. "This isn't fair. I want to wear my costume and be the star of the Christmas pageant. I want to be with my dad and open presents on Christmas morning."

Kathleen tried to encourage her. "Come on, Lucy. You'll still get your presents. Just on a different day."

Kathleen's encouraging words had the opposite effect on Lucy as she began to sob heavily. Kathleen was at a loss. She looked toward Sam for rescue.

Sam placed his hand on Lucy's shoulder and said, "Hey, let's take it one day at a time. Okay, kiddo?"

Lucy looked up at him and wiped away some tears. Sam smiled.

Lucy tried to put on a brave face and said, "Okay, but it'll take a miracle to save this day from stinking."

Kathleen chuckled to herself, and Lucy asked, "What?"

Kathleen answered, "I totally agree, but I think I might be having my very first kid-friendly idea."

Lucy was not convinced. "That would be a miracle."

Kathleen was too pleased with her break-through idea to worry about Lucy's mumbling. She jumped to her feet and commanded, "On your feet, troops. Operation: Save This Day From Stinking has just begun."

Chapter Eighteen

he sun shone down brightly that afternoon. It lit the entire city of Tulsa with prisms of light as it glistened off the ice in the trees and the drifted snow that blanketed everything in sight. Although it was still below freezing outside, the sun made everything feel warm and glow with energy.

Kathleen wasn't sure if the winter storm was long gone or if this was just a brief respite with more snowfall to follow. In any event, she was undaunted.

The gauntlet had been thrown down, and she was determined not to let her Operation: Save This Day From Stinking fail.

Sam and Lucy were bewildered as they watched Kathleen scurrying through the house, garage, and attic, collecting items of clothing. Even though they didn't know what she was up to, their spirits were lifted with a sense of anticipation.

Finally, Kathleen got everything and everyone ready and ushered them into her back yard.

As they stood there observing the winter wonderland around them, Kathleen glanced at Lucy. She was bundled up in a motley collection of oversized, cast-off garments. Her ensemble was topped off by a furry hat with flaps covering her ears.

Lucy looked down and said, "Look at me. I look like I shrunk."

Kathleen responded encouragingly, "You look adorable, doesn't she, Sam?"

Sam smiled and nodded. "Quite fetching."

Lucy's eyes widened, and she grabbed the earflaps on her fur hat, pulling them away from her head. "I look like a dog."

Sam laughed uproariously, but Kathleen tried in vain to cover her mirth and smiles.

Lucy playfully scolded them. "Hey, people. You're supposed to be cheering me up."

Kathleen surveyed the back yard and took charge of the situation, commanding, "Okay, okay. Follow me. Ready?" Without further explanation, Kathleen fell onto her back in the snow and started making a snow angel.

Lucy squealed and shouted, "Oh! Snow angels! I love snow angels!"

She turned and fell back onto the snow next to Kathleen and began making her own snow angel. Sam looked on with a smile on his face.

Lucy looked up and said, "Come on, Sam."

Kathleen chimed in, "Yeah, Sam. Jump in."

Sam looked around dubiously. "I don't think so."

Lucy challenged him. "Why not? You chicken?"

"Yeah, Sam. You chicken?" Kathleen prodded. "Or maybe you're a chicketarian."

Sam was bewildered and looked at Kathleen questioningly.

Lucy rolled in the snow and roared with laughter. "Chicketarian. I can't believe you said that."

Lucy and Kathleen continued to laugh at Sam and taunt him mercilessly. Lucy jumped up and began tugging on Sam's arm. "Just try it. I want to see what you look like as an angel."

Sam had a faraway, wistful look in his eye for a moment, then he gave in and finally turned and fell back into the snow. The other two cheered as they sat and watched Sam lying in the snow.

Kathleen looked down at Sam. "Okay now. Don't disappoint the little girl."

Lucy added, "Yeah. Don't disappoint me."

"Oh, all right. Here we go," Sam said, resignedly.

Sam gave in to the moment and began flapping his arms and legs, creating his own snow angel. Lucy and Kathleen lay down next to Sam and began making more snow angels.

Lucy called to Kathleen, "Your yard is gonna look just like heaven."

Kathleen shot back doubtfully, "Until the snow covers it."

Lucy rolled over onto her stomach and tossed a snowball at Kathleen. Lucy scolded Kathleen like she had heard her teachers do, simply by calling the name of someone misbehaving. "Kathleen!"

Kathleen laughed and replied, "Sorry, but it's true."

Sam turned to Lucy and said playfully, "You could teach her a thing or two about imagination."

Lucy thought for a minute and then replied, "I don't know, Sam. Some people just lose it when they get old."

"Old! Who are you calling old?" Kathleen scooped up some snow and tossed it at Lucy.

Lucy responded by picking up some snow herself and challenged, "Then prove it!"

Lucy threw her snowball at Kathleen and took off running across the back yard. A gleeful snowball fight ensued, with Sam, Kathleen, and Lucy all participating energetically until they were thoroughly exhausted and the sun began to duck behind the trees and houses in the west.

As the afternoon seemed to get suddenly colder without the help of the sun beating down on them, they knew it was time to go back into Kathleen's house where they were effectively trapped and cut off from the outside world. This fun and outrageous romp in the snow in the back yard had given them each a wonderful respite from all of the challenges they had been dealing with.

Kathleen's plan for Operation: Keep This Day From Stinking had certainly worked wonders.

There are certain moments and certain days that are forever locked in our memories. They represent special times, places, and people that we capture in the scrapbook of our minds. Just a fleeting thought of these memories can bring us back to that special time and place as well as the emotion we felt when we were there.

Sam, Kathleen, and Lucy each knew that they would never forget that special afternoon playing in a Christmas snow.

Chapter Nineteen

ntil a person has been without modern conveniences and climate control for a few days, it is easy to forget how much the outside temperature fluctuates. Twenty-first century houses, offices, and other buildings are kept livable and even habitable through modern heating and air conditioning technology.

The cold from the snow storm was starting to work its way into Kathleen's house. After Sam, Lucy, and Kathleen came in from their snow angel artwork and ensuing snowball fight, they were having a hard time getting warm again.

Sam knelt in front of Kathleen's gas fireplace and clicked the automatic igniter. Sam wasn't familiar with this newfangled thing, but he kept at it until the gas ignited.

He smiled and said, "Ah, there we go. Nothing like a nice warm fire."

Lucy propped her feet up in front of the fire and wiggled her striped toe socks.

Sam glanced at her and asked, "How about those toes? Are they thawing out?"

Lucy nodded and replied, "Yeah. They're getting better." She sighed contentedly and gazed into the fire. After a few moments, her brows furrowed.

Kathleen approached from the back of the sofa with an armload of blankets. She spread one over Lucy. "Then how come you sound so distressed?"

Lucy said with all the maturity and sincerity she could muster, "I don't want to be a complainer, 'cause all of a sudden you're being really nice."

Sam tried not to smile and struggled to keep a straight face.

Lucy continued. "I just wish my dad was here. That's all. We were supposed to go to the Christmas pageant tonight. I'm the star."

Sam had a sudden brainstorm and sat up with a twinkle in his eye.

He said, "Hey! What's stopping us from having the Christmas pageant tonight?"

Lucy looked at him disdainfully and replied, "I think your brain is still frozen. Remember, snow storm of the century?"

Sam remained determined and said emphatically, "If the Christmas pageant was supposed to happen tonight, then, by golly, it should happen tonight!"

Lucy and Kathleen caught Sam's infectious enthusiasm, and they started believing something special could really happen in that house that very night. The three bustled about frantically and, within a matter of minutes, had turned Kathleen's dining room into a theatrical sceneshop. The table was covered with an eclectic mix of household odds and ends, the props and costumes for a Christmas pageant. On the top of the counter was a silver tray with graham crackers, chocolate, and marshmallows.

Kathleen was working at the gas stovetop, making a simple meal of soup and grilled cheese sandwiches, while Sam and Lucy worked on the Christmas pageant. As Kathleen bent down to put the cheese back in the cooler, she noticed that she had glitter stuck to her arm. She tried to wipe it off, but it was no use.

Usually, that would have been enough to upset Kathleen, as she wanted everything in her world to be impeccable and orderly, and that included herself, first and foremost.

But now Kathleen just shrugged it off as she heard Lucy announce from the other room, "The performance will begin in two minutes."

Kathleen dished out their soup and sandwiches hurriedly and put the plates on a silver tray. She carried the tray quickly into the living room.

As Kathleen entered the living room, she noticed that it had been magically transformed into a dinner theatre. Sheets had been strung up as curtains, and candles had been gathered from all around the house for "stage lighting."

As Kathleen set the tray down, she could hear rustling behind the curtains. Lucy's voice could be heard saying, "Places! Places everyone!"

Kathleen settled into her place on the sofa and surprisingly paid no attention to the mess surrounding her. Her eyes twinkled brightly like a child on Christmas morning as she eagerly awaited the show.

Chapter Twenty

here are a number of elements in the world that create universal excitement in the hearts and spirits of young and old alike. Among these elements are kids, live plays, the Christmas holidays, and ancient stories filled with wisdom and hope. All of these elements were present in Kathleen's living room that had been converted to a theatre that night.

As the show began, Sam suddenly appeared from behind the curtain. He paused dramatically, and with all the dignity he possessed, announced, "The story you are about to see is one hundred percent true. And one hundred percent interactive."

Sam gave Kathleen a wink. Lucy's hand stuck out from the curtain, offering Sam a note. Lucy cleared her throat, and Sam took the note and read, "The Christmas Pageant has a big star, the lovable Lucy Wright."

Lucy popped her head out from behind the curtain and nodded graciously. She said theatrically, "Thank you. Thank you. Please, no. Really."

Lucy gave the applause sign with her hands. Kathleen finally took the cue and began clapping. Lucy nodded and acknowledged the applause saying, "Thank you. You're too kind."

Sam continued his curtain announcement. "And now for the feature presentation." He disappeared behind the curtain and quickly reappeared with a sheet rigged on his head like a shepherd. He pulled out a small, worn book, its pages curled from gentle use. The book fell open to a familiar passage as Sam cleared his throat.

Lucy passed through, carrying a sign that read, *The Olden Days.*

Sam began to read. "In those days, a decree went out from Caesar Augustus that all the world should be registered."

Lucy's voice could be heard offstage providing sound effects. "Cha-ching." Lucy's sound effects startled Sam and took him by surprise. Kathleen stifled a laugh.

Sam gathered his composure and continued. "And so, Joseph went to his hometown of Bethlehem to be registered with his betrothed, Mary, who was with child."

Lucy appeared from behind the curtain. She had a pillow stuffed in the front of her shirt to create the theatrical aforementioned pregnancy. She was carrying a broomstick that had a paper plate attached to it with a face drawn on it that was playing the part of Joseph. The "couple" waltzed across the stage and disappeared behind the curtain.

Sam continued the narrative. "And while they were there, the time came to give birth. And so, the Virgin Mary gave birth to her first-born son and wrapped Him in swaddling clothes and laid Him in a manger, because there was no room for Him in the inn."

Lucy appeared from behind the curtain with a plastic clothes basket and the doll from Kathleen's closet wrapped in a small blanket. She gently placed the "baby" in the basket and again disappeared behind the curtain.

Sam continued. "Meanwhile, in a nearby field…." He flashed behind the curtain and reappeared with a puff of cotton in his hand. He knelt down and began to pat the cotton. It was obvious that he was a shepherd tending his flock.

Lucy provided sound effects from offstage. "Baaaaaa. Baaaaaa."

Sam spoke to his unruly sheep. "Oh, you settle down, Nicodemus."

Lucy, offstage, continued providing the sounds of sheep. "Baaaaaa. I'm a girl sheep. My name is Fluffy."

Sam corrected his error, "My mistake, *Fluffy*."

Suddenly, Lucy appeared in her glittery, angelic glory. She shined a flashlight into Sam's eyes and said, "Don't look into the light."

Sam responded, "Who are you? I'm terrified."

Lucy comforted him. "Don't be afraid. I'm an angel."

Sam inquired, "A real angel?"

"Don't ask questions. I'm here to announce a joyful event to you. To the world, actually. A child has been born in Bethlehem, and He is the Savior of the world. 'Messy-ah' and Master of the World."

Lucy mispronounced Messiah, but Sam corrected her pronunciation by saying, "Where can I find the Messiah?"

Lucy forgot she was playing an angel and spoke directly to Sam. "Bethlehem. I already said that."

Sam whispered something to Lucy, prompting her. She immediately spoke as the angel. "Oh yeah. Look for a baby wrapped in a blanket and lying in a manger."

Lucy paused, but then thought of something else to say. "And look for me. I'll be the star. And whenever you're feeling lost or sad, just think of me and hum this tune."

Sam gave her a stern look, and she got back on track, saying, "I mean, peace be to all, and to all a good night."

Lucy flashed a peace sign and exited the stage humming the tune to "Twinkle, Twinkle, Little Star."

Kathleen applauded enthusiastically.

Lucy re-emerged from backstage holding a sign that read: *End Act One*.

Chapter Twenty-One

othing can take us away from our daily trials and tribulations or suspend reality like a theatrical performance.

If only for a brief time, Kathleen, Sam, and Lucy had been transported thousands of miles across the ocean, and centuries back in time. This provided an oasis in the turmoil they were dealing with through the snowstorm that had paralyzed their lives and that of everyone in the city. Their spirits were lifted, and hope filled Kathleen's living room that had been converted into a dinner theatre.

Kathleen and Lucy were seated on the floor with blankets over them.

Sam spoke to them. "There is a part to the story that has become very special to me. I would like to read it if that is okay."

Kathleen and Lucy simultaneously nodded *yes* as they continued eating their dinner that was spread out on the coffee table in front of them.

Sam opened a worn traveler's Bible and said, "And when the time came for Mary and Joseph to present the child to the Lord, they took baby Jesus to the temple. In Jerusalem, at the very same time, there was a man, Simeon by name, a good man. And God's Spirit was upon him. And God revealed to him that he would see the Messiah before he died. Led by the Spirit, Simeon went to the temple, just as the parents of Jesus brought the child to be presented before God. And Simeon, seeing the baby, took Him into his arms and he blessed God, saying 'God, You can release Your servant; release me in peace as You have promised; with my own eyes I have seen Your salvation, and now it's in the open for all to see.'"

Sam looked up at his audience of two, tears glistening in his eyes. It was obvious that the words he was reading had deep meaning for him.

He continued, "A Light for all the world."

As he read, Lucy was cradling the theatrical baby from the play in her arms. Kathleen self-consciously wiped a tear from her eye, impacted emotionally by everything going on around her that evening.

Kathleen spoke to Sam. "I have never heard that part of the story before."

Sam nodded and confirmed, "It has become very special to me."

Lucy got another blanket from the sofa and wrapped it around her. The three of them settled in comfortably on the floor and watched the fire flickering in front of them.

Suddenly, Kathleen popped up and exclaimed, "Oh, wait! I almost forgot." She rushed out of the room.

In less than a minute, Kathleen returned with an array of items she spread out before them. In a few moments, Sam, Lucy, and Kathleen were holding coat hangers, with all of the ingredients to make S'mores on a tray beside them.

Sam announced to no one in particular, "I love S'mores."

Lucy said, "I've always wanted to do this!"

They began working diligently to straighten out their hangers.

Kathleen turned to Lucy and inquired in shock, "You've never had S'mores?"

Lucy explained, "I've had S'mores, but my dad makes them in the microwave." She impaled a marshmallow on her coat hanger and extended it into the flames.

Kathleen was finding it hard to imagine that Lucy had never had this experience. She responded, "That's criminal."

"My dad doesn't trust me with fire." Just then, Lucy's marshmallow burst into flames. Lucy tried to remain calm but spoke nervously, "Um… Help!"

Kathleen grabbed Lucy's coat hanger and blew out the flames. Lucy stared at the charred remnants of her marshmallow.

Sam came to the rescue. "Here, I'll trade you." He offered his golden brown marshmallow to Lucy and took the burnt one for himself.

Lucy looked at him in shock. "Really?"

Sam smiled and took a bite out of Lucy's marshmallow that had been burned black.

Lucy and Kathleen exclaimed in unison, "Ew!"

Sam, with his mouth full, looked at them questioningly. "What?"

"It's burnt!" Kathleen explained.

"And ashy," Lucy chimed in.

Sam remained undaunted. "I like 'em burnt."

Lucy rejected his notion. "No way. Not for me. I like mine just like this."

"I have to agree with the kid," said Kathleen. "Crisp outside and gooey on the inside. No campfire flambé for me."

Lucy appeared thoughtful. "Flambé. I think that's my new favorite word."

"What's your old favorite word?" asked Kathleen.

Lucy thought for a moment and replied, "I'd have to say...persnickety."

Kathleen nodded. "That makes sense."

Lucy shot back, "Hey! You're the most persnickety-ous person I ever met."

Sam sat back and let out a belly laugh.

It was a joyous time for the three unlikely souls stranded together in an unexpected Christmas snow; but just like the weather in Oklahoma, the world can change very quickly.

Chapter Twenty-Two

deep cold fell over the entire city that night. The sky was clear, and the full moon made the snowscape below look surreal.

The winter storm had been a two-edged sword for the community. On one hand, it had paralyzed travelers and forced everyone to seek shelter. On the other hand, it had given friends and family, as well as some unexpecting souls, a unique opportunity to experience a new perspective on the holiday.

Sam's laughter rang out through Kathleen's house.

She glared at him and asked indignantly, "What are you laughing about?"

Sam looked at Kathleen and Lucy, observing, "You two are just alike."

The two looked at one another. Lucy turned toward Sam and stared incredulously. "Us? You're crazy."

Sam shrugged. "Yeah. You're probably right."

Lucy squinted her eyes in his direction. "I know that trick."

"Trick?" Sam questioned.

Lucy nodded. "The one where you real quick pretend to agree so I'll stop talking."

Sam just shook his head and laughed out loud.

Kathleen said, "I invented that trick."

"That trick has been around long before your years," Sam argued.

Kathleen nodded but shot back, "Fine. Then I perfected it."

Lucy turned toward Kathleen and asked poignantly, "How come you always want to be perfect?"

The question seemed to disarm Kathleen. She mumbled, "Um, I don't know how to answer that."

Lucy confronted her. "Well, how about the truth? My dad says you should always tell the truth."

"You won't let me off the hook, will you?"

"Say it, Kathleen. I try to be perfect because..."

Kathleen shifted, pulling the blanket more tightly around her. She spoke uncomfortably. "I guess...I want people to like me."

Lucy laughed while Kathleen looked surprisingly insecure.

Sam sensed the discomfort building. "Lucy."

Lucy felt Sam's admonition and responded, "Sorry. It's just that I like the 'not perfect' Kathleen so much better."

Kathleen eased up a bit and let out a deep sigh.

Sam looked at Kathleen as he considered Lucy's statement, finally saying, "I'd have to agree."

"Yeah, but you're like a saint," Kathleen responded. She turned her gaze from Sam to

Lucy. "And you're still a kid. You have no idea what life is really like."

Lucy sat up straight. "Okay. First of all, I know a lot about life, because I'm really smart. And second of all, I've been seeing a therapist since I was eight."

"Which means?"

"I know about feelings, and I'm good at tracing them."

"What?" Kathleen could not comprehend the conversation she was having with this 10-year-old child.

"You need to find your root, Kathleen," Lucy stated emphatically.

Kathleen was shocked and confused. "My what?"

"Your root. It's usually like your worst day ever. Like the moment you knew you were always going to be different."

Kathleen stared at Lucy in disbelief.

Lucy probed further. "So...do you know it?"

"Well, yeah," Kathleen stammered.

Lucy mimicked her therapist, "Do you want to talk about it?"

"Not really." Kathleen closed down.

"It figures."

"What?" She couldn't believe this child wouldn't let it go. "This from the expert. You're hardly the poster child for all this."

Sam interrupted, trying to play the role of the peacemaker. "Ladies..."

Lucy continued. "Hey, at least I'm trying to deal with my issues."

Kathleen stared at Lucy. "Issues? Seriously? You're 10. When are you going to let go and move on with your life?"

Lucy wore a pained look on her face, and Kathleen knew she had gone too far. At once, she felt remorse that she had allowed her own pain to emerge as a weapon to injure an innocent child.

Lucy announced with finality, "It's getting late. I should be in bed." She stood up, on the verge of tears.

Kathleen tried to stop the inevitable. "Lucy, wait."

Lucy ignored her. "Thank you, Sam, for a wonderful evening." Lucy turned her gaze toward Kathleen. "And thank you, Kathleen, for ruining it." She stormed down the hall, and the sound of the slamming door seemed as loud as an avalanche.

Chapter Twenty-Three

he silence was deafening. Kathleen and Sam were left alone by the gas fireplace, but Lucy's presence could be felt as if she were still in the room.

Kathleen felt both hurt and embarrassed. She had effectively reopened her own old wound while poking and prodding Lucy's wound that had not yet healed. Kathleen didn't know what to say, so she began absentmindedly straightening up the living room.

She said to no one in particular, "Ugh. Look at this place."

Sam tried to reassure her, more about the confrontation than the state of the living room, "It's not that bad."

Kathleen, thinking as much about the situation with Lucy as the living room, said, "It's a mess."

Sam looked around the living room and said playfully, "It suits you."

Kathleen started to protest but then admitted, "You know...you're right. Only, I can't seem to straighten myself out. And not for lack of trying."

"Sounds tiring," Sam said thoughtfully.

Kathleen nodded. "Exhausting. I think I get it all worked out, but then the smallest thing happens, and I'm right back there."

Sam looked at her questioningly. "Where?"

Kathleen felt as if she were walking a tight rope a million miles above the earth as she blurted out, "Watching my dad leave."

She paused, trying to organize her thoughts, and then she plunged ahead. "I was only 10, but I've lived it so many times. And I always feel the same. Alone."

"Where was your mother?" Sam asked. "Was she gone, too?"

"My mother? No, she was very much there."

"You don't get along?"

Kathleen tried to simplify her complex situation, saying, "We used to. Then she remarried."

"Bad guy?" he asked.

Kathleen admitted, "No. He was fine. But he's not my dad. I didn't want a new family, as hard as he tried to change that."

She moved back to the sofa and settled down onto it. "I blamed my mom for anything and everything I didn't like about my life. I moved out as soon as I could. Now the only one around to blame is me."

Sam tried to encourage her, "You won't get anywhere blaming yourself."

"Everyone says that."

"Because it's the truth."

Kathleen explained, "The truth is, my dad didn't care about me. Not enough."

Sam focused his world-weary but wise eyes on her. "How can you know that?"

Kathleen walked over to the window and looked outside. The snowscape she was seeing was not the one outside her window but, instead, it was the scene of 30 years ago on that fateful night.

She spoke. "I was there when he left. I've lived it so many times. We had just decorated our Christmas tree, and it was just…beautiful. Simple, but perfect. So, there I was, lying under the tree, when my dad came rushing down the hall and right out the door. He didn't see me, so I knocked on the window, and he stopped. He looked right at me. But then he just turned and walked away."

Kathleen was lost in the emotions of that long ago night.

Sam interrupted her memories. "Have you ever tried to get in touch with him?"

Kathleen turned her attention from the window and spun back toward Sam. "Why? He's the one who left. He could find me if he wanted."

Sam spoke as the voice of experience. "It's not always that simple."

Kathleen stared into his eyes, looking for answers.

Sam broke the silence, admitting, "Your story could just as soon be mine."

"Your dad leave you?" Kathleen questioned.

Sam sighed heavily and spoke words laced with guilt. "No, it was me who did the leaving, sorry to say."

Kathleen considered Sam in a new light. "How could you do that?"

Sam let his memories wander back along a rough and rocky road. "It's complicated. My own dad was messed up. I didn't want a thing to do with him; but then as I got older, I started my own family. The funny thing is, I turned out just like him. The temper. The drinking. The women. It devastated my wife. I loved her. I loved my family, but I couldn't bring myself to change. So I left."

"You gave up."

"It was the worst day of my life. I walked around for years like a failure. And I earned the title. Lived up to it for years. But I wanted to change."

"What was stopping you?" Kathleen confronted.

"I told myself it was too late. Didn't think I deserved it. Then I met this young man who told me it wasn't too late. He said there was hope for me, and I wanted it to be true. He invited me over for dinner with his family, and he showed me..."

Sam pulled out the worn traveler's Bible and lovingly traced its edges with his hand. "The thing I'd been looking for my entire life. A chance at forgiveness. A chance to change. And right then and there, I was Simeon. You heard words in the story like 'salvation.' Well, I experienced it. It was like a light went off, and it lit up my entire world. It changed everything."

Sam slowly set the Bible down on the coffee table and looked toward Kathleen on the sofa. His eyes were moist.

Kathleen gazed into those eyes as she considered his words. She sensed that there might be some significant answers available to her, so she asked, "Did you go back to your family?"

"No. Not yet. I'm working on that one."

Kathleen protested, "But you said you changed."

"And that's true," Sam admitted. "Everything about me had changed. Situations haven't. I'm sorting through a lifetime of bad decisions."

She searched his wise gaze and asked, "Do you think I should look for my father?"

Sam answered with certainty as if he had considered this question many times. "Some things in life are worth seeking out. Family's one of them."

Kathleen got up with a noncommittal shrug and began to blow out the candles. "I don't know. I would think that if he wanted to see me, he would seek me out."

"What about your mother?"

Kathleen sighed heavily. "Oh, I don't know about that. I think forgiving her really would take an act of God. We haven't talked in years."

She paused for a moment to collect her thoughts. "It's funny, though. She still calls me every Christmas. I usually don't answer. Just listen to the message."

Sam suggested, "Maybe you should talk to her."

"I don't know."

He looked at her. "And you never will if you don't try."

Kathleen sighed with exhaustion. "Let me sleep on it for a night…or ten."

Chapter Twenty-Four

It was very late on that bitterly cold night. The outside remained frigid from the Arctic wind that blew across the frozen snow. The inside of Kathleen's house seemed frozen from the thoughts, feelings, and memories that both Sam and Kathleen had uncovered.

Sam silently made his way into the guest room while Kathleen slowly walked down the hall to her bedroom. She opened the door, stepped inside, and eased the door shut behind her, leaning against it for a moment to collect herself. She started to lock the door but reconsidered and left it unlocked.

In the moonlight that filtered through the blinds, Kathleen could see Lucy sprawled out across her bed, once again taking up all of the available space. There was a tangle of sheets and blankets.

Kathleen stealthily moved around the bed and gently reorganized the bedding to create a barrier of pillows and blankets between Lucy and herself. Finally accomplishing this, she leaned back in the bed and wearily sighed. As she closed her eyes and experienced her first moment of rest, Lucy's hand extended over the barrier of pillows and smacked Kathleen squarely in the face.

Even the most bitter cold night is eventually and inevitably followed by a new day. The sun shone brightly on Kathleen's house that next morning. Icicles glistened and dripped from the rooftop.

Kathleen awoke on the floor once again. She did not remember leaving her bed and retreating to the floor, but she knew it must have happened shortly after the sleeping Lucy **had** struck her.

The sun shining on Kathleen's face through the blinds gave her hope for the new day. She saw that her bed was an utter mess, and Lucy was gone.

As Kathleen slowly walked down the hall, she passed her guest bathroom and noticed Lucy standing at the counter looking into the mirror and putting in barrettes.

Kathleen stopped and said, "Good morning."

Lucy responded automatically and unemotionally, "Good morning, Kathleen."

Kathleen stepped into the bathroom doorway and watched Lucy struggle with her hair for a few moments. Then she moved behind Lucy and began brushing the young girl's hair.

Kathleen looked at Lucy's reflection in the mirror. "You have such beautiful hair. You should wear it down."

Lucy looked into the mirror and responded, "My dad says it's just like my mom's."

"I bet she was beautiful," Kathleen replied.

Kathleen paused for a moment, took a deep breath, and plunged in, "Hey, I wanted to talk with you about last night. I'm sorry."

Lucy focused on Kathleen's eyes in the mirror. "Me, too."

Kathleen lightened the mood, observing, "We're quite a pair, aren't we?"

Lucy nodded and confided, "Yeah. My therapist says I act bad sometimes 'cause I'm afraid I'll get left out."

Kathleen empathized with Lucy. "You mean by your dad?"

"He gets so busy with work," Lucy explained. "And then he always wants to see you. My dad likes you. A lot."

Kathleen tried to reassure her. "Well, your dad loves you. A lot. And that's not something everyone can say."

Lucy shrugged as Kathleen continued to brush her hair. "Kathleen, how come loving people's so scary?"

Kathleen spoke with more certainty than she felt. "I guess 'cause you can't make 'em love you back."

Lucy nodded and agreed. "Yeah, and you don't want 'em to leave you out."

"Yeah, that's the scariest part," Kathleen echoed.

Out of the blue, Lucy asked, "Do you love my dad?"

Kathleen was silent and stopped brushing Lucy's hair. She spoke softly. "I think I'm too scared to say."

Lucy pointed at Kathleen's ring finger and predicted, "Well, I think he's going to love you real soon."

Kathleen smiled, almost embarrassed as she felt a flood of emotion wash over her.

Tears appeared in Lucy's eyes as she implored, "Can you make sure he doesn't forget about me?"

Kathleen knelt down next to Lucy so she could look directly into her eyes, saying, "Look here. That would never happen. Not to you. You're as unforgettable as they come."

Kathleen pulled Lucy into a warm embrace. For the first time, the two connected and were willing to let the walls between them down.

Kathleen said, "Come on. Let's get your hair done and get some breakfast."

Lucy smiled.

As Lucy's hair fell into place, so did the feelings and emotions between them. They both knew that they had crossed some invisible barrier and had found a new place. There would be bumps in the road ahead, but somehow Kathleen and Lucy understood they would be walking that road together.

Chapter Twenty-Five

hristmas celebrations, decorations, and festivities come in all different shapes and sizes. Some are ornate and magnificent. Others are simple and humble. Regardless of the size, grandeur, or expense, what makes a Christmas celebration significant is the heart, meaning, and soul behind the holiday.

As soon as Kathleen and Lucy entered the kitchen, Sam could tell that there had been a transformation between the two of them. The night before, there had been a vast, insurmount-able gulf. That morning, Kathleen and Lucy seemed like sisters or kindred spirits. Obviously, an immense healing had begun.

As Kathleen entered the breakfast nook carrying her plate of food, Sam and Lucy were already busy devouring their bacon and egg breakfast. Partially in honor of the festive season, and partially due to the reconcilia-tion between Kathleen and Lucy, the bacon and eggs had been arranged on each plate to create a smiley face, with eggs as eyes and bacon the mouth.

Sam was thinking how wonderful it was to be spending time with a 10-year-old, because it gives adults the opportunity to do child-like things that adults want to do anyway but too often avoid because of the status and demeanor that society demands of maturity.

Lucy shoved a huge piece of bacon into her mouth.

Kathleen said, "Okay, wait a second. I thought you didn't eat bacon."

Lucy sat up and immediately appeared defensive. "Who said I..." Suddenly, she remembered the dinner several nights ago at Kathleen's restaurant. She knew she had been caught red-handed.

She admitted, "Oh, yeah. Chicketarian." She smiled sheepishly. "More like persnicketarian."

Kathleen laughed and said, "You're a good kid." She winked at Lucy, reassuring her that it was all in good fun.

Lucy addressed both Sam and Kathleen. "Do you know what today is?"

Kathleen feigned ignorance. "Wednesday."

Lucy tried to steer the conversation in another direction. "Well, yeah. But besides that."

Sam picked up on the game and offered, "Garbage day?"

Lucy became frustrated with the adults' inability to grasp what was obvious to her. She corrected them. "Guys, it's the eve of Christmas Eve!"

Kathleen spoke as if she had just remembered something very important. "How could I have forgotten?"

"I don't know about you guys, but in the real world," said Lucy, "I would be making a ginger-bread house."

Kathleen threw out an objection. "Problem."

"What?" Lucy asked.

"I just used the last of the eggs."

Lucy failed to understand the obstacle. "Eggs?"

"For the gingerbread."

Lucy confidently dismissed Kathleen's objection. "My gingerbread house usually comes out of a box. Do you have one of those?"

Kathleen looked solemn and shook her head *no*.

Sam took that moment as his opportunity to save the day. "I'm no expert, but when I was a boy, we made some pretty nifty houses out of graham crackers and candy."

Lucy picked up on Sam's solution and added brightly, "We have graham crackers."

Sam looked toward Kathleen to deal with the next obstacle. He asked, "Got any candy?"

Kathleen nodded hesitantly, then turned and opened the cupboard door. There was a tidy row of organic foods and cooking supplies revealed inside. Kathleen reached way in the back of the cupboard and took out a container labeled Flax

Seed and another labeled Spelt Flour and one more labeled Mangosteen.

Lucy was bewildered and certain Kathleen had lost her mind. She pointed to the containers and asked, "What's all of this?"

"You'll see." Then she directed Lucy, "Arms out."

Lucy extended her arms, and Kathleen began loading her up with the containers from the cupboard. When Kathleen had handed Lucy the final container, she motioned, and they moved back to the table.

Lucy was more certain than ever that Kathleen had developed some type of mental problem. She asked dubiously, "Flax seed?"

"Open it."

Lucy opened the container labeled Flax Seed to reveal a rainbow of gumdrops inside. She looked at Kathleen sternly. "I'm telling my dad about this."

When she opened the other two containers, they were filled with licorice and chocolate pieces. Sam and Lucy laughed uproariously as if having caught Kathleen with her hand in the cookie jar or, in this case, the candy dish.

Kathleen knew she was caught. "Okay. So I have a little bit of a sweet tooth."

Lucy corrected her. "*I* have a sweet tooth. *You've* got a problem."

Kathleen shot back, "You're going to have a problem if you don't hush."

Lucy turned toward Sam and said conspiratorially, "This explains a lot."

"This is my secret stash," Kathleen said. "You should be thanking me."

"None for me," Sam stated. "I've sworn off sweets."

Lucy responded enthusiastically, "Good. Then I get to have yours." She shoved a gumdrop into her mouth with gusto. They all laughed.

Lucy began laying out graham cracker walls as Kathleen mixed powdered sugar and water to make frosting.

Lucy looked up from her project and asked, "Hey. What time is it?"

Sam pulled out his pocket watch, "Ten o'clock."

Lucy nodded and declared, "Oh, good. We're right on schedule."

Kathleen asked, "You have a schedule?"

"More of a To Do List," Lucy explained.

Sam looked at Lucy. "And what exactly do you need to do?"

Lucy gestured toward the gingerbread house. "This, of course. But we also need to make Christmas wish lists, decorate the living room, and play a game of hide-and-seek."

Sam declared, "Well, I'll be…"

"What?" Lucy asked innocently.

"Those are the exact things I wanted to do today," Sam responded. "How did you know? Was I talking in my sleep?"

Lucy laughed. "Stop teasing me, Sam."

"Well, I guess this was all just meant to be," Sam said meaningfully.

Kathleen nodded and agreed, "I guess you're right."

Chapter Twenty-Six

ver the next few hours, Kathleen's living room was transformed into a Christmas village. Kathleen, Sam, and Lucy each performed their tasks with relish. The time flew by, and at Lucy's direction, the hour arrived for the previously-announced game of hide-and-seek.

Sam could be heard throughout the house, counting, "Eight... Nine..."

The ruffle on Kathleen's bed fluttered as Lucy and Kathleen concealed themselves under the bed.

As Sam called, "Ten," with finality and announced, "Ready or not, here I come," Lucy whispered to Kathleen under the bed, "I'm nervous."

Kathleen cautioned, "Shhh. You're gonna give us away."

The door slowly opened into the bedroom. Lucy quietly whispered, "He's coming!"

From beneath the dust ruffle, Lucy and Kathleen could see Sam's shoes appear next to the bed as Sam searched through the room. Lucy clapped her hand over her mouth in suspense, but she felt relief as Sam passed their hiding spot and walked away.

Lucy whispered to Kathleen, "He's leaving."

As Kathleen watched Sam's shoes retreating as he moved away from the bed, her mind once again was transported back many years. She was observing other shoes step away as she watched her father walk through their house and out the front door.

Young Kathleen confronted her mother. "He's leaving." She tried to read her mother's face. "He's coming back, right?"

Kathleen's mother took a ragged breath and said, "No, honey. I don't think he's coming back this time."

Young Kathleen accused her mother, asking, "What did you say to him?"

Kathleen's mother tried to explain the unexplainable. "Katie, honey, you have to understand. This is what's best for both of us."

Kathleen persisted. "How could you just let him leave?"

Kathleen's mother turned toward her and moved to give her a hug. Kathleen cringed and rejected her mother as she turned away. As Kathleen's mother reached out to grab her arm, the grown Kathleen's thoughts returned to the present as Sam reached under the bed and grabbed her arm.

Sam lifted up the dust ruffle, declaring, "You're it!"

Kathleen was startled, both by her mental return to another place and time as well as by Sam's discovery of their hiding place.

She exclaimed, "Oh!"

Lucy said, "Ah, man. He scared you." She turned toward Sam, asking, "How did you know?"

Sam revealed his secret. "A little too much giggling under there."

"That had to be Kathleen," said Lucy. "I'm like a ninja hider."

It was Kathleen's turn to count while Sam and Lucy found places to hide. She sat down on the sofa in the living room and began calling, "One… Two… Three… Four… Five…"

Kathleen heard a familiar door rattling, followed by a loud thump. She smiled in recognition, certain she knew where she would find one of the hiders.

Kathleen warned, "Careful," as she continued counting. "Six… Seven… Eight… Nine… TEN." Then she got up, certain of her direction, and walked down the hall. She called, "Okay. I'm coming."

Kathleen stealthily made her way down the hall, glancing into each room she passed on her way toward her destination. The door to the storage closet stood open a crack. Kathleen whipped open the door with anticipation and cried, "Gotcha!"

No one was there, but several of the items stored in the closet had been knocked from their shelves and were jumbled on the floor.

"Hmm."

She picked up one of the overturned boxes. As she lifted the old, dusty box, one of the flaps popped open, revealing some long-forgotten Christmas decorations from her childhood tree. As she glanced inside, she noticed the ornament that hung above her the night her father left—a white porcelain angel. Kathleen was taken back by the memory of the angel. She was overwhelmed with emotion and sat down on the floor in the storage closet.

She studied the special ornament lying in the box and remembered the place of honor where it had hung on her family's tree when she was a child. Kathleen pulled the angel out of the box by its hook and held it above her head. A peaceful smile crept onto Kathleen's face. Holding the porcelain angel above her head provided the same perspective she had viewed many years before as she lay under the Christmas tree. Kathleen closed her eyes and remembered that long-ago time and place.

She was jarred back to the present when she heard Lucy's voice calling, "Hey!"

Kathleen opened her eyes and saw Lucy standing in the doorway.

"I'm supposed to be the one hiding."

Lucy noticed the faraway look on Kathleen's face. "Are you sad?"

Kathleen responded with certainty, "No. Actually, I'm good."

Lucy admired the porcelain angel that Kathleen was still holding. "That's pretty. It looks like our snow angels."

Kathleen considered for a moment and said, "Oh, yeah. I guess it does."

"Is it your guardian angel?" Lucy inquired poignantly.

Kathleen was taken aback. "Huh. I guess you could say that."

Lucy gave her a big hug, and Kathleen allowed her arms to fall around the young girl's shoulders.

"It's good to know someone's looking out for you, don't you think?" Lucy had summed up the encounter.

Kathleen agreed with those words on many levels. "Yes, I do."

Chapter Twenty-Seven

athleen had rediscovered the porcelain angel ornament; and in doing so, she had rediscovered a lot of memories and emotions.

She couldn't help but think about that Christmas tree 30 years ago where that ornament had been lovingly hung in a special place. She remembered the joy of looking at the angel hanging there, and she recalled her last memory of that special ornament as she lay on the floor looking up through the Christmas tree branches at that special angel.

That was just before her father walked out of the house and out of her life. He had taken not only her hopes and dreams but any joy she would feel toward Christmas trees and Christmas for decades to come.

Kathleen and Lucy were just preparing to leave the storage closet when they unexpectedly heard a knock at the door. They looked at one another in surprise, and then Lucy raced down the hall to discover who was knocking.

As Lucy approached the front door, she could hear Sam's muffled voice from outside. She could discern his distorted image through the frost-covered glass in the front door. As Lucy opened the door, she could see that Sam was carrying something over his shoulder.

Sam bellowed, "Ho! Ho! Ho!"

Lucy shouted, "It's Sam!"

Kathleen could hear them at the front door. She carefully replaced the porcelain angel back in its box with the other Christmas decorations and put the box back on the shelf in its place.

As Kathleen entered the living room and approached the front door, she heard Sam repeat, "Ho, Ho, Ho. Merry Christmas!"

Sam was coming through the front door with something that looked like a large branch.

Lucy declared, "A Christmas tree!" She was jumping up and down with excitement as Sam tapped the base of the tree on the front porch, knocking the snow from the branches as he entered. Snow fell off the tree onto the package that had been delivered days before and remained unnoticed on the front porch.

Kathleen looked at Sam skeptically, "It looks more like a branch than a tree."

Lucy was undaunted. "A Christmas branch!"

Sam took off his wet and snowy shoes and left them on the front porch next to the forgotten package.

He moved into the living room carrying his branch, where he began arranging it in front of the picture window. He assessed the situation and said, "I'm going to need a pot, some string, and about 15 minutes of uninterrupted man time."

"Man time?" Kathleen questioned dubiously.

Lucy raced toward the kitchen, shouting, "I'll get the pot!"

Kathleen shrugged, "I guess I'll get some string."

As Kathleen entered the kitchen, Lucy was rummaging through the cupboards. She turned and held up two identical pots and questioned, "Which one?"

Kathleen tried to assess the situation. "What do you think?"

Lucy indicated one of the two identical pots, and stated with certainty, "This one."

Kathleen nodded and agreed. "My thoughts exactly." She opened a drawer and pulled out a spool of cooking twine.

"You keep rope in a kitchen?" Lucy scrunched up her face.

Kathleen explained in a matter-of-fact tone, "For tying up turkeys, chickens, nosey children. You know…"

Lucy reprimanded Kathleen, "You need an attitude check." She turned and carried the pot she had selected toward the living room, and Kathleen followed with string in hand.

They noticed Sam had cleared a spot in front of the picture window. Lucy placed the pot on the floor, announcing, "Pot."

Kathleen chimed in, "String," as she handed the string to Sam.

They stepped back and watched Sam as he measured out a piece of string the right length for his project. He stopped in the middle of his labors and turned toward them questioningly. "Ladies?"

Kathleen said, somewhat mockingly, "That's right, man time, excuse us." They again headed for the kitchen, leaving Sam to his business.

There, they also began working, creating decorations for the Christmas tree with all manner of items they discovered in Kathleen's kitchen.

As Sam finished securing the tree in place, Lucy and Kathleen emerged from the kitchen, bearing their homemade decorations. They shooed Sam away, declaring it was their turn to make a contribution toward the Christmas tree project.

Sam retreated into the kitchen in search of a cup of coffee and a bit of rest as he looked forward to the transformation that was going on in the other room.

Chapter Twenty-Eight

athleen and Lucy worked feverishly in the living room on the makeshift Christmas tree.

In the kitchen, Sam relaxed, sipped his coffee, and waited for the unveiling of the Christmas tree with great anticipation. Finally, Lucy called "Okay, Sam. You can come in now."

As Sam walked toward the living room, Lucy was beside the Christmas tree admiring their handiwork. Paper clips had been linked together to create a shiny garland. Tea bags had been covered in glitter to make sparkling orna-ments. The newspaper containing Kathleen's review had been cut up into ribbons and then looped together to create a paper chain.

As Sam stepped into the living room, he questioned, "Girl time's over so soon?"

Lucy called back, "We like to get things done."

When Sam got his first good look at the tree, he declared, "I'll say you get things done! That is the most beautiful Christmas tree I've ever seen."

As Kathleen entered the living room from the hallway, she announced, "One more thing…" She walked across the room carrying the angel ornament and carefully placed it on the tree.

Lucy looked at Kathleen gratefully and declared, "Perfect."

The trio began decorating the rest of the living room to match the festive Christmas tree. Sam turned on the gas fireplace and Kath-leen hung her mismatched knee-high stockings on the mantle above the "Gingerbread" village. She lit several candles on the mantle and then placed one candle on the floor illuminating the gingerbread house.

Sam created the image of a wrapped Christmas package on an Etch A Sketch. He placed it under the Christmas tree next to an old Lite-Brite toy, also displaying the image of a Christmas gift.

He looked beneath the tree at the Etch A Sketch and then said to Kathleen, "Just hope she doesn't shake it to see what's inside."

Kathleen muttered, "Hmm."

Sam settled onto the sofa, enjoying the warmth of the fireplace as he admired the tree. Lucy re-entered the living room carrying her backpack.

Sam declared, "Mighty fine work there, girls."

Lucy acknowledged Sam's praise, but then solemnly announced, "There's only one thing left to do."

Kathleen sighed in exhaustion and sat on the sofa next to Sam. She turned to Lucy. "Relax?"

Lucy shook her head emphatically, "No! Wish lists for Santa."

"Of course," Kathleen replied. "How could I have forgotten?"

Lucy took charge. "Don't worry. I've got it under control. Everyone just relax."

Sam and Kathleen sat up on the sofa as Lucy distributed customized papers and markers.

Kathleen looked at the paper she'd been handed. Lucy had written *Kathleen's Christmas Wish(es)*. Lucy had drawn little pictures of an angel, a shovel, and a cell phone around the top.

On Sam's page, Lucy had written *Sam's Christmas Wish(es)*. She had drawn pictures of a lollipop, "Fluffy" the lamb, and a burnt marshmallow.

Lucy explained, "I made them especially for you."

Kathleen looked at her page and commented, "They're very nice."

Sam glanced at his page and declared, "Best gift I've gotten in a long time."

"Then you definitely need to fill out your wish list," Lucy replied.

She sat down and began filling out her own list. She wrote down numerous items including a pony and a popcorn machine. She glanced up and realized that Sam and Kathleen were not filling out theirs. She asked, "Don't you want anything?"

Kathleen shrugged. Sam shook his head and said, "There's only one thing I really wanted... but at this point, it looks like only the good Lord could arrange it."

Lucy demanded, "Then write it down."

Sam replied, "I don't think it will make any difference." Kathleen looked on, her interest piqued.

Lucy glared at Sam, declaring, "I'll be the judge of that, mister."

Kathleen sensed that Sam was upset. She interceded, asking, "What is it, Sam?"

Sam sighed and set down his pen. He reached into his pocket and pulled out his pocket watch, which he looked at tenderly. Sam had a faraway look in his eyes.

"My great-grandfather was a jeweler. He made this watch by hand. It's one of a kind."

"I don't get the wish," said Lucy.

Sam studied the watch and explained, "It was my Christmas wish that I'd get to give it to my daughter this Christmas."

Kathleen spoke, "I'm sorry, Sam. Is that why you were catching the bus?"

Sam nodded. "Yup. I was finally on my way to finding her."

Lucy looked down at her paper. "Write it down, Sam. Christmas is only two days away. A whole lot of hopes and prayers can come true before then."

Sam smiled, picked up his pen, and began writing on his list. He paused, and carefully put his watch back in his pocket and said, "It's just complicated, that's all. But you're right. Anything can happen."

All three of them began thoughtfully writing on their Christmas wish lists. Their mood was abruptly broken when unexpectedly the lights and television came back on. In the bright artificial light, what had seemed like a magical candlelit Christmas setting just a moment before, now looked more like a pathetic mess.

Kathleen hopped to her feet and asked, "Anybody seen the remote?"

She began tidying up the remnants of yesterday's dinner theater. Lucy looked on with disappointment as Sam began folding up blankets. He discovered the television remote control buried between two sofa cushions.

Lucy looked at the two adults and asked, "What are you guys doing?"

Kathleen took the remote from Sam and turned the TV to the weather channel. "Getting things back to normal," she responded.

Stubbornly, Lucy reached over and turned the TV and lights off, which returned the living room to its previous cozy, festive state. "I don't like normal."

"But you're getting what you wanted," Kathleen argued. "You'll be home for Christmas."

Lucy blurted, "What if I don't want what I wanted?"

"That's called a mid-life crisis," Kathleen replied.

Lucy flopped back onto the sofa. "Mid-life? But I'm too young to die!"

Kathleen and Sam just looked at one another.

Kathleen said, "I should call your dad. See if he has any news about his flight. Where's the phone?"

Lucy ignored her and buried her face in a pillow. Kathleen said emphatically, "Lucy."

Lucy's voice was muffled in the pillow. "What?"

"I need to plug your phone in so I can use it."

Lucy sat up and declared, "It's off limits."

Impatiently, Kathleen said, "C'mon, Lucy, don't start this." She reached over and turned the lights back on.

Sam encouraged Lucy. "You don't want your dad to be alone for Christmas, do you?"

His question changed Lucy's mood and the mood in the room.

Lucy pointed and said, "In my backpack. It's all there."

Kathleen grabbed the phone and left the room. Lucy looked at Sam and said, "I feel weird inside."

He nodded and said, "Yeah, me too, kiddo. How about you and I get this place cleaned up?"

Lucy and Sam reluctantly set about cleaning up Kathleen's living room and putting everything back in order.

Chapter Twenty-Nine

he next morning, the power was back on throughout Kathleen's neighborhood. Neighbors were digging out their driveways and cleaning the snow and ice off their cars.

From the kitchen, Kathleen called, "Breakfast's ready."

Lucy rushed in and took a seat in the breakfast nook. Kathleen slopped oatmeal into a bowl.

"Oatmeal?" questioned Lucy unenthusiastically.

Kathleen stepped over to the table, poured syrup on top of Lucy's oatmeal, and then set the bottle on the table. "With maple syrup?"

"Do you have brown sugar?" Lucy tentatively asked, as Kathleen turned on the coffee grinder, drowning out her question.

Kathleen declared, "I can't hear you!"

Lucy shouted just as the coffee grinder noise ceased, "What's your rush?"

Kathleen hurried through her breakfast preparation. "Your dad's flight lands in an hour. We still have to dig out, and then I have to get myself to the restaurant to set up for the lunch rush. So eat up."

As Kathleen turned on the coffee grinder again, Sam entered, carrying his briefcase and overcoat. He set them aside and took a seat at the table. Lucy glanced at Sam, not liking the looks of things. Kathleen put a French coffee press on the table. "The coffee will be ready in a minute."

Lucy turned to Sam and interrogated, "Where do you think you're going?"

"I've got a bus to catch."

"Did we discuss this?" Lucy asked.

"I didn't know it needed discussing."

Lucy called to Kathleen imploringly, "Kathleen…"

Kathleen rushed over, carrying coffee mugs, then rushed back to the refrigerator for milk. She returned to the table and poured milk into each of their oatmeal bowls.

Lucy repeated, "Kathleen." Kathleen looked toward her. "Sam thinks he's leaving."

Kathleen paused in her breakfast preparations and turned to Sam, "Did we talk about this?"

Sam shrugged and stammered, "Well, in all the rush…"

Lucy declared, "People need time to prepare for things like this, Sam."

Sam raised his eyebrows. "Things like…?"

Lucy interjected, "Good-byes."

Kathleen glared at Sam and asked, "When were you gonna tell us?"

"Now, I guess," Sam sighed.

Lucy rolled her eyes and blurted, "Men."

Sam tried to defend himself. "Never been too good at good-byes."

Kathleen said, "Well, how about you make it up to us?"

"How?" Sam questioned.

Lucy echoed, "Yeah, how?"

"How about...you stay?"

Sam sighed and leaned back in his chair. Lucy confronted him, "Yeah, how about it?"

Kathleen justified their position, "Storm's only moved past us, Sam. Roads are supposed to be worse outside of town."

"It's Christmas Eve, Sam," said Lucy. "You don't want to spend Christmas on a bus, do you?"

"Even I wouldn't do that," said Kathleen, making her final argument.

Sam paused and finally offered, "I suppose... I could stay."

Lucy enthusiastically asked, "For Christmas?"

Sam replied uncertainly, "For a little while longer."

The other two cheered and gave each other a high five.

Lucy exclaimed, "You're gonna get to meet my dad and my parakeet." She paused, remembering something. "Oh, no!"

"What?" Kathleen asked.

"How long can a parakeet live without food? And water...and heat?"

Kathleen diverted the question. "Um, we'll have to ask your dad when we pick him up at the airport." Then she glanced at her watch. "Yikes." She took a last bite and announced, "Five minutes until departure."

As Kathleen rushed around the kitchen, cleaning and putting everything away in the aftermath of breakfast, Lucy got her backpack and headed for the car. Sam followed her into the garage. As Lucy got into the passenger seat, Sam opened the garage door and began cleaning the remainder of the snow and ice away with what was left of Kathleen's broken shovel. As Kathleen rushed out of the house with her car keys, Sam was standing beside the open garage door.

Kathleen said, "Okay, now we really need to get going." She opened the driver's side door and slid behind the wheel.

Kathleen called to Sam, "I'll be back for you at five o'clock sharp."

Sam questioned, "Five o'clock?"

"We'll go straight to the restaurant from here, so..."

Lucy leaned over Kathleen and continued, "Come hungry! She's a great cook."

Sam saluted and called, "Yes, Ma'am." He set the broken shovel beside Kathleen's door, then tipped his hat as Kathleen backed the car out of the garage and into the street. As Kathleen and Lucy disappeared from sight, Sam thoughtfully paused for a moment, then closed the garage door and went into the house.

He began doing some more cleanup in the kitchen but was interrupted when Kathleen rushed through. Sam asked, "What are you…?"

Kathleen interrupted his question explaining, "Forgot Lucy's phone." She rushed past Sam again and headed back for the garage, carrying the cell phone and charger.

Kathleen called, "Bye, Sam."

Sam walked into the living room and looked out the picture window in time to see Kathleen hurriedly walk out of the garage and toward the car parked in the driveway. He knocked on the glass. Kathleen turned toward the sound, saw Sam in the window and smiled. Kathleen waved and then got into her car and drove away.

As they drove along the slushy street, Lucy handed her a picture she had drawn. At a stoplight, Kathleen unfolded the paper to reveal three stick figures.

Kathleen exclaimed, "Look at you, you're quite an artist."

Lucy asked, "Can you tell who it is?"

"It's me, you, and Sam. Right?"

Lucy corrected her, "No, silly. It's me, you, and Daddy." She picked up her pencil and drew a heart between the two taller stick figures. "See?"

Kathleen nodded. "Oh yeah. Now I see it."

Lucy smiled as Kathleen took the pencil and quickly drew on the paper, then handed it back. As Kathleen drove through the intersection, Lucy looked down at her picture and saw that Kathleen had drawn a heart between the other two figures, which represented the two of them.

Chapter Thirty

s Kathleen negotiated the entrance onto the freeway that would take them to the airport, she was experiencing many emotions. Kathleen was not used to feeling emotions, as she had blocked them out of her life for many years. She was coming to understand that, in order to feel the joy of her new relationships and the healing taking place, she also had to deal with pain, anger, and unforgiveness from her past.

The snow along the freeway was piled higher than she had ever seen in Tulsa, but all the lanes of the freeway were clear to the airport.

Kathleen and Lucy felt the excitement building in the car as they approached the Tulsa airport terminal. Kathleen pulled up to the curb near the arrivals door and hoped that Andrew would emerge before airport security forced her to move away from the curb.

Lucy cheered as her dad stepped through the automatic doors from the baggage claim area and strode rapidly down the sidewalk toward their waiting car.

A limousine driver who was parked in front of Kathleen called to Andrew. "Do you need a limousine, sir?"

Andrew shook his head and joyously called out to the limo driver, "No, my girls are right over there."

Lucy jumped out of the car and ran directly to her dad, leaping into his arms for a big hug. After a bear hug, Lucy took his carry-on roller bag and rolled it to the back of Kathleen's car, which gave Andrew and Kathleen a private moment for their reunion. Lucy stood near the trunk of the car, smiling at Kathleen, and gave her a quick, knowing wink.

Andrew caught the small exchange and felt grateful that there had obviously been some kind of breakthrough between his daughter and Kathleen. Andrew lovingly hugged Kathleen.

After Andrew's bag was stowed in the trunk, Lucy rushed to get into the back seat, leaving the front seat for her dad and Kathleen. The three of them all talked at the same time as they drove away from the airport.

It was a joyous reunion, and the love that Kathleen, Andrew, and Lucy felt was very strong and full of potential.

Kathleen found that many areas of her life needed to be reconsidered in light of the recent revelations that had been given to her. It seemed natural for her to want to celebrate the Christmas season in a festive way.

She eventually found herself back at the supermarket where she had met Sam. As she approached the checkout counter carrying two large poinsettias, the Santa on the counter displayed a sign reading: *1 Day Until Christmas.*

The same store clerk she had encountered just a few nights before was at the register. He wore the now-familiar Santa hat, and he eyed Kathleen suspiciously.

She smiled brightly and put a dollar in the container for the children's fund.

The store clerk seemed relieved and filled with Christmas cheer. He wished her a heartfelt "Merry Christmas" as she walked out of the store carrying the poinsettias.

Kathleen drove to her restaurant, where she was excited to display her new Christmas cheer and wondrous new outlook on life.

As Kathleen walked into the front door of her restaurant carrying the two large poinsettias, all of her employees and several customers did a double take. It wasn't unusual to see Kathleen walking into the restaurant, and it wasn't unusual to see someone carrying poinsettias on Christmas Eve, but the combination of the two was something they had never before experienced.

After Kathleen set the poinsettias down on the counter and greeted everyone with the spirit of the season, she walked toward her office.

She moved a chair away from one of the tables so she could stand on it to attach Martin's mistletoe over her doorway.

Martin rushed over to get a closer look, uncertain of Kathleen's unusual behavior. As he stopped by her side, she bent down from her perch atop the chair and kissed Martin on top of his bald head. Martin let out a hearty laugh as a crowd of employees and patrons gathered around, applauding.

Kathleen then began moving throughout the room, greeting everyone with Christmas wishes and season's greetings. She spotted the food critic seated at an out-of-the-way table in a corner. As she walked toward the table, several of the employees and patrons looked on with concern. They were relieved when Kathleen stopped at the counter, picked up one of the poinsettias, and presented it to the food critic.

As Kathleen set the plant on his table, she cheerily said, "Merry Christmas!" The food critic gave her a warm and sincere smile.

Martin and Claud looked on in shock and amazement.

As Kathleen finished her rounds, greeting all of her patrons with heartfelt Christmas wishes, she was surprised to see how late it was getting.

She thought, *Time goes by really quickly when you are enjoying people and the holiday season.*

She rushed out of the restaurant and drove toward her house to pick up Sam for the dinner they had planned.

As Kathleen pulled into the driveway in front of her house, the clock on her dashboard read 4:58 P.M. She smiled as she got out of the car. She had made it with two minutes to spare.

Chapter Thirty-One

s Kathleen rushed along the sidewalk in front of her house and bounded up onto the porch, her thoughts were of Sam. He had become one of the most significant and influential people in her life, and she had only known him a few days. She had learned so much from him, or more accurately, he had helped her discover things in her mind, heart, and spirit that had been hidden away for many years.

She was looking forward to introducing Sam to Andrew at a wonderful dinner that evening.

As she opened her front door, Kathleen noticed the soggy, weather-worn package lying on the porch next to her door. She picked it up and carried it inside.

As Kathleen called out to Sam, she noticed how waterlogged the package had become. "You better be ready, because... Ew!" She passed through the living room and dropped her bag and the soaked package on the counter.

Kathleen knew Sam had to be somewhere in the house, so she called out to him again. "You better be ready, because I'm going to change so fast, you're not going to..."

She noticed the living room had been totally cleaned up and put back into its original condition, except for the Christmas tree and the stockings hung over the fireplace.

She continued yelling to Sam, "...believe it!"

Kathleen was struck by how different the living room looked since Sam had thoroughly cleaned it and put it back in order. She was amazed he had accomplished this in the time she had gone to the airport, the supermarket, and her restaurant.

She said to herself and Sam, wherever he was, "You cleaned up."

She turned to look in the kitchen. It, too, was spotless, but Sam was nowhere in sight.

Kathleen slowly approached the guest room and peeked inside to no avail. The bed had been made, and everything was clean and orderly, but Sam was not there.

Kathleen returned to the living room and called, "Sam?"

She glanced at the Christmas tree and, for the first time since returning home, she noticed two pieces of paper attached to the tree. She rushed over to look at them, but they were only the wish lists Lucy had given to her and Sam. Kathleen confirmed that her wish list was still blank as she had not written anything on it the previous night. As she looked at Sam's wish list, she noticed that he had written on his list.

Kathleen removed Sam's list from the Christmas tree and settled onto the sofa. Sam's wish list read: *To see my daughter again.*

Kathleen looked up at the Christmas tree, and the sight of the porcelain angel both comforted her and gave her courage. She promptly stood up and walked purposefully into her office.

Kathleen pulled out her laptop computer and set it on her desk. She opened a search engine and stared at her computer screen for a moment with her fingers poised above the keyboard. Kathleen took a deep breath and typed in: *MITCHELL, ALBERT.* She looked at the words and added the initial *S.* and *Minnesota* and then hit the enter key.

She scrolled down, stopping at a result for the *San Diego Tribune.* She clicked on the link which opened the city's obituaries. It read: *S. Albert Mitchell, age 73, born August 31, 1937, in Scandia, Minn., went to be with the Lord December 19. He will be greatly missed by his new friends at Town Chapel.*

Kathleen blankly stared at the computer screen. She thought about all the things she had lost and everything she had found.

Just then, from her purse, her cell phone began ringing. Thankful she had remembered to retrieve it from the restaurant, she reached for the phone. The caller ID announced it was Andrew. She answered as she continued staring at the computer screen.

She heard Lucy's voice questioning, "Hello… Kathleen… are you there?"

Kathleen snapped out of her reverie long enough to say, "Oh, uh… Hi, Lucy. Yes, I'm here."

"Where are you? We're at the restaurant."

"Oh, Lucy, honey. I'm sorry. I should have called you. I'm sorry, something's come up. I'm not going to make it tonight. Can I talk with your father, please? Thanks, honey."

Kathleen gave Andrew the barest of explanations, pleaded for his understanding, and promised she would explain more to him later.

Chapter Thirty-Two

athleen sat on the sofa in front of the fireplace and thought about her father's obituary that she had just read. She absentmindedly pulled a gumdrop from the Christmas village that sat beside the fireplace. Without thinking, she popped the candy into her mouth. She grimaced, and quickly spit it out and threw it into the fireplace.

Normally candy was a comfort and refuge for Kathleen, but tonight, not even candy could help her.

Kathleen slid down onto the floor and sat with her back against the sofa. She glanced up at the Christmas tree, looking directly at the angel. Kathleen began to cry.

That night, Kathleen slept fitfully and awoke disturbed and out-of-sorts. She went into her autopilot mode and performed her morning ritual without thinking.

She jogged through the neighborhood and passed the park without even noticing her surroundings. She blended a breakfast drink and somehow consumed it without tasting it. She got dressed for the day and went through her obligatory teeth-whitening routine in a mindless stupor.

Finally, she went into her home office to pack up her computer and get her phone. As she was reaching for her computer bag, she noticed the message light indicator blinking on her phone. It showed that she had 15 messages. She pushed the button for her messages to play and then hit *speaker* so she could hear them as she worked.

The phone announced, *Message one, Thursday, December 24, 6:57 P.M.*

She heard her mother's voice. "Katie? It's Mom. Call me, please. It's important."

The phone announced, *Message two, Friday, December 25, 6:05 A.M.*

She heard her mother's voice again. "Katie, please. It's about your father."

Kathleen sank into her chair as the message continued. "I really didn't want to tell you this in a message, but…Katie, your father passed away last Monday. I have been trying to get…"

Kathleen bolted upright, grabbed the phone and turned it off. She flinched at her own immaturity, but she wasn't ready to deal with it.

She rummaged through her desk drawers absentmindedly and discovered the lollipop Lucy had tasted earlier and rewrapped. Kathleen gagged at the disgusting taste and tossed it into her trash can.

Picking up her things, she rushed out of her office, through the living room, and was headed for the door when she noticed the soggy package sitting on the counter.

She stopped, set her bag on the floor, and picked up the package.

Kathleen tried to read the outside label, but it was smeared from all the moisture. She tore into the water-soaked package with ease. Inside, she discovered a soggy envelope from the Law Offices of Stovall-Gundersen-Trost-Winters-Jestus, Stafford, PA, and an unmarked padded envelope.

She opened the envelope from the lawyers, but the ink had run, and she could only make out her own name. She turned her focus to the padded envelope and opened it.

Inside was a small black box with a folded white note attached to it with a rubber band. Scratched on the outside were the words: *For Katie With Love, Dad.*

Kathleen smoothed out the note and placed it gently on the counter. She removed the rubber band from the box and slowly opened it. Inside was an eerily familiar hand-carved gold pocket watch.

Kathleen looked around the room and called, "Sam?"

No one was there. She placed the box back on the counter with shock. She sat down in a chair and stared at the box.

She reached into the padded envelope again to discover a plastic padded envelope. She opened it to find the small, worn Bible that Sam had read from.

Kathleen flipped through the pages, scanning the highlighted and underlined passages. On the front, inside cover of the Bible, she discovered an inscription written to her. There was a list entitled: *My Gifts for Katie.*

Kathleen's feet tapped nervously as she read the list that had been thoughtfully and lovingly written for her. She slowly shut the Bible and held it close to her chest.

Kathleen knew what she had to do and she committed to do it as she heard the words her father had written for her ringing in her head. As she went into her bathroom to pack things for an overnight stay, she heard the words her father had written, *My final gifts for Katie by S. Albert Mitchell.*

Kathleen walked into the living room and reached to take the porcelain angel off of the tree as she heard her father's words, *The gift of faith. That you would have a love for God in your heart.*

In her bedroom, as Kathleen was packing her overnight bag and placing the angel inside, she heard her father's words, *The gift of friendship. That you would learn to love others deeply.*

Kathleen was in her seat on the airliner with discarded packages of peanuts strewn across the tray table as she held her father's worn Bible and heard his words, *The gift of peace. That you would enjoy life to its fullest and have a heart filled with peace.*

As the taxi cab pulled up in front of Kathleen's childhood home, she paid the driver and got out as she heard her father's words, *The gift of family. That you would embrace family. No matter the circumstance.*

As the cab pulled away, Kathleen walked up the pathway toward the house, holding the small Bible in her hand. In her mind, she heard more of her father's words. *And most of all, the gift of forgiveness. That you would discover the healing and restoring power of forgiveness.*

Kathleen reached the doorstep and tucked the Bible into her purse with care. She folded her hands and stood motionless for a moment, working up the courage to knock. Finally, she knocked once and then again. She was about to knock for a third time when she saw the door-knob turn, startling her. The door opened a crack but stopped short.

She heard her mother's voice calling to someone in the back of the house. "No. Four-twenty-five. I said to preheat the oven to four hundred twenty-five degrees."

As the door slowly opened, Kathleen saw her mother standing before her. She was struck by the fact that her mother looked pleasant and attractive. Her mother spoke, not yet recognizing Kathleen.

"I'm so sorry about…"

Her mother stopped short, and she and Kathleen stared at one another.

Kathleen blurted, "Hi, Mom."

Her mother simply replied, "Katie." Her eyes were filled with hurt, sadness, and confusion, but then she noticed tears forming in Kathleen's eyes.

Kathleen stammered, "I hope…I hope I'm not too late."

All the years of hurt, anguish, and conten-tion melted away, and Kathleen's mother took her daughter into her arms.

Kathleen's mother reassured her. "No, baby. You're right on time."

They embraced for a few moments, then Kathleen's stepfather, Bill, walked into the room. Not knowing who was at the door, he called to his wife, "Honey, I think you should see this."

As Bill approached the front door, Kathleen noticed his hair had grayed over the years, and he was wearing a floral apron and oven mitts. He was holding a casserole dish in his hands.

He asked, "Is it supposed to bubble over like…" When he noticed the two teary-eyed women on the doorstep, he exclaimed, "Uh-oh." He glanced at his wife, trying to discern the cause of her tears.

Kathleen said, "Merry Christmas, Bill."

Bill exhaled in relief, saying, "Oh, thank God. Happy tears." Motioning with his casserole, Bill said, "Come inside, both of you. Do you have any bags?"

Kathleen gestured toward her carry-on and answered, "Just this one. I've got it, thanks."

She followed Bill and her mother through the front door. As they reached the front entryway of the family home, Kathleen's mother began sniffing the air. She looked at Kathleen and questioned, "Is something burning?"

Kathleen just nodded.

Her mother exclaimed, "Bill, I told you... bless his heart, he's a good man, but he's a mess in the kitchen. Forgive me."

Kathleen watched her mother scurry down the hall toward the kitchen. She could hear Bill and her mother talking.

Her mother said, "Honey, just put that down. Let me help you."

Kathleen smiled as she looked around the house, taking in the sights as if she were a stranger. In some way, she was seeing her childhood home for the first time.

She walked into the living room toward a Christmas tree that sat next to the picture window, just as it had many years before. She reached into her purse and took out the porcelain angel. She hung it on the Christmas tree in its rightful place.

As she looked at the angel hanging where it had been that Christmas so long ago, her feelings and emotions began to build. She looked toward the picture window and then closed her eyes and let go of a lifetime of bitterness. She spoke aloud, "I choose to forgive."

When Kathleen opened her eyes, she looked through the picture window just as she had done as a child. She noticed the image of Sam across the street. Sam looked into her eyes, and the distance between them and the years of pain seemed to disappear.

Kathleen reached into her purse and grabbed the pocket watch. She held it up to the window for Sam to see. He smiled and said, "Merry Christmas, Katie."

Kathleen replied, "Merry Christmas, Daddy."

The two of them shared a special moment of knowing as they looked into each other's eyes. Then a city bus passed on the street between them, and Sam was no longer there; but for Kathleen, it was more than enough.

Chapter Thirty-Three

he following year brought many changes into Kathleen's life and, consequently, into the lives of her family and friends. Like all changes that people experience, some of them were painful, while others seemed to come naturally.

Kathleen's relationship with Andrew deepened and became more comfortable. Andrew was able to get to know the real Kathleen as she got to know herself.

Lucy came to love and trust Kathleen, not as a replacement for her mother, but as a new figure in her life she could respect, trust, and look up to.

Kathleen visited her mother and stepfather, Bill, several times and spoke with them on the phone regularly. They had a lot of time to make up for, and they were each committed to forming a real family.

As the next Christmas approached, Kathleen's staff and restaurant customers noticed an amazing transformation. *Kathleen's Ti Amo's Restaurant* became a holiday showplace and a Christmastime favorite for diners.

Kathleen's staff enjoyed their boss's new holiday spirit. She hosted a special dinner for all the employees and their families on December 23, and then announced that the restaurant would be closed throughout the Christmas holiday. This news was met first with shock, then gratitude, and finally applause and hugs.

Kathleen's family gathered at her home for Christmas Eve.

Lucy announced to everyone, "It's a lot different this year with the power on and everyone here except..."

Lucy stumbled over her words, and Kathleen took over, saying, "Yes, Lucy. You're right. It's wonderful to have heat, lights, and all of our family...and in a very special way, Sam is here, too."

Everyone looked at the glorious new Christmas tree in front of the picture window. It was nine feet tall with an unimaginable array of lights and decorations, but right in the center of everything hung the little porcelain angel.

Lucy said, "I guess our guardian angels are always with us."

Kathleen, her mother, and Bill prepared a wonderful Christmas feast in the kitchen while Andrew and Lucy planned and worked in the living room.

After dinner, Lucy ceremoniously announced, "It's time for the Christmas pageant, and I'm the star."

After everyone gathered in the living room, Lucy theatrically proclaimed, "The story you are about to see is one hundred percent true...and one hundred percent interactive."

Lucy was a year older but still had all of her spunk intact. Kathleen's mother proved to be a real scene-stealer, and there were cameo appearances by Andrew and Kathleen. Bill was an appreciative and enthusiastic audience throughout the performance.

As the play drew near the end, Kathleen took out her father's worn traveler's Bible and read the familiar passages that tell the story of the very first Christmas.

As she finished her dramatic reading, she sat down on the sofa and gazed at Sam's wishes for her, lovingly inscribed on the inside cover of the Bible. Over the past year, she had tried to understand those wishes, and tried to make them part of her life.

Sam's first wish for her was that she would have the gift of faith and have the love for God in her heart.

Kathleen had always understood God in a religious way from her childhood training, but over the past year, she had begun to understand God in a relationship way. God was someone who was part of her daily life and part of all of her thoughts and feelings, not just someone she thought about during religious holidays at church.

Although Sam had wished many things for Kathleen, and Kathleen was beginning to wish more for her own life, she had come to understand that her relationship with God was central to everything else in her life.

As Kathleen sat and read the next words her father had written on the inside cover of the Bible, she understood his next wish for her was the gift of friendship, and that she would learn to love others deeply.

Although Kathleen's relationship with Andrew and Lucy had grown far beyond a friendship, she now understood that the friendship they had initially built was the foundation for the deeper relationship she wanted to have with both of them for the rest of her life.

Kathleen had grown to understand friendship in new ways. She now understood that, in order to have a friend, she needed to be a friend. Her relationship had deepened with many of her colleagues and patrons, so that she now could count them among her friends, and she knew many of them considered her a valued friend.

The year had taught Kathleen that the word *friend* means more than someone whose name you know and with whom you exchange greetings or pleasantries. Friendship means caring about other people and getting involved as a significant part of their lives.

Kathleen read her father's wish that she would enjoy life to its fullest and have a heart filled with peace.

Kathleen had come to realize that peace wasn't simply the absence of conflict or turmoil; but, instead, peace was an abiding, knowing, and understanding deep within a person. Kathleen was learning how to control her anxieties and the resentments that had made her life so empty in the past. She was taking more time for herself and more time to simply read and reflect.

Ironically, Kathleen found that she was actually able to get more done and run her business more efficiently while enjoying her life in a new, peaceful way.

Her father had wished that she would receive the gift of family and that she would embrace family, no matter the circumstance. This had been difficult for Kathleen, since her father, who was trying to teach her about family, had been the initial catalyst for the dysfunctional family feelings she had endured for decades.

Kathleen had come to understand that all families are flawed because they are populated with flawed people. She knew she had to do her best to bring as much love, peace, and joy to the family as possible while accepting each family member for who they were and where they were in their lives.

Kathleen was beginning to know that nothing can bring the same joy or heartbreak as a family.

Finally, Kathleen's last wish from her father was that she would embrace the gift of forgiveness and discover its healing and restoring power.

Kathleen had struggled mightily with forgiveness. She had learned that the hardest person of all to forgive was herself, and unless she could begin by accepting forgiveness, she could never give the gift of forgiveness to others.

She had laid this burden down, but found that forgiveness was an ongoing process, as we are often tempted to revisit old feelings and wounds.

As Kathleen surveyed the joyous holiday scene of her family enjoying Christmas in her home, she thought about the many Christmas wishes that had come true, and the many more she wanted to give and receive in Christmases yet to come.

Each ensuing year, as the holiday season approached, she felt a new joy and wonder that she had never before experienced. Christmas would never again be just an obligation or a burden. Instead, it would be a special time with friends and family to celebrate gifts received and given.

Each time Kathleen saw snowflakes drifting down from above, she thought about that amazing Christmas snow that had brought her father back to her, along with many new gifts in her life. Someone had told her that every snowflake was special and unique. She would always think of the snow in that way, but she knew she would never forget the first time she truly experienced unconditional love, forgiveness, and a Christmas snow.

About the Author

Jim Stovall is the author of 16 books including the best-seller *The Ultimate Gift*, which was also a major motion picture from 20th Century Fox, starring James Garner, Brian Dennehy, and Abigail Breslin.

He is among the nation's most sought-after motivational and platform speakers. Despite failing eyesight and eventual blindness, Jim Stovall has been a national champion Olympic weightlifter, a successful investment broker, and an entrepreneur. He is the founder and president of the Narrative Television Network (NTN), which makes movies and television accessible for America's 13 million blind and visually impaired people and their families. NTN's program guide and samples of its broadcast and cable network programming are available at www.NarrativeTV.com.

The Narrative Television Network has received an Emmy Award and an International Film and Video Award among its many industry honors.

Jim Stovall joined the ranks of Walt Disney, Orson Welles, and four U.S. presidents when he was selected as one of the Ten Outstanding Young Americans by the U.S. Junior Chamber of Commerce. He has appeared on *Good Morning America* and CNN, and has been featured in *Reader's Digest*, *TV Guide*, and *Time* magazine. The President's Committee on Equal Opportunity selected Jim Stovall as the Entrepreneur of the Year. In June 2000, Jim Stovall joined President Jimmy Carter, Nancy Reagan, and Mother Teresa when he received the International Humanitarian Award.

Jim Stovall can be reached at 918-627-1000.